G000122729

The Queen of a Distant Country

Suddenly, in his middle thirties, Tom Metfield realizes he is
turning into a recording machine. More and more his personal
experience is becoming just raw material for his novels.
Tom's answer is to look at Miranda, the solicitor's wife
who queens it over the literary set in the Yorkshire seaside
town where he spent his youth. Miranda was, to use her own
expression, a Name once. What has made her settle for
infinitely less than she could have achieved? In exploring
Miranda's character, Tom, reluctantly, finds himself
exploring his own.

JOHN BRAINE

The Queen
of a
Distant
Country

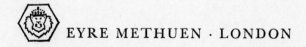

EYRE METHUEN · LONDON

First published *1972*
Copyright © John Braine (Bingley) Ltd *1972*
Printed in Great Britain for
Eyre Methuen Ltd
11 New Fetter Lane, London EC4P 4EE
by Butler & Tanner Ltd
Frome and London

SBN 413 44840 1

Praising, that's it! As a praiser and blesser
he came like the ore from the taciturn mine.
Came with his heart, oh, transient presser,
for men, of a never-exhaustible wine.

Voice never fails him for things lacking lustre,
sacred example will open his mouth.
All becomes vineyard, all becomes cluster,
warmed by his sympathy's ripening south.

Crypts and the mouldering kings who lie there
do not belie his praising, neither
doubt, when a shadow obscures our days.

He is a messenger always attendant,
reaching far through their gates resplendent
dishes of fruit for the dead to praise.

RAINER MARIA RILKE
The Sonnets to Orpheus: First Part
Trans. J. B. Leishman
Courtesy St John's College, Oxford
and The Hogarth Press

One

The point at which it all starts is when Deirdre walked –
or rather ran – out of my house. To be precise, it was a
fine morning in late May, and she left my bed at 7am and
left the house at 7.20am.

'You don't love me,' she screamed. 'You don't love anybody. You only ever wanted me for one thing and now
you don't even want that.'

She was wrong; looking at her naked body with its small
breasts and big nipples and the bush of red pubic hair as
big as my hand I was overpowered by an erection which
almost hurt.

If she had put her hand there, then she wouldn't have
left the house. And I would have gone to her cottage in
Suffolk with her. She didn't; so I lay back, my eyes half-
closed, and watched her dress; this seemed to intensify the
erection, but I was determined to endure it. Miranda
had entered my mind again. That was the reason why I
couldn't go with Deirdre to her country cottage as I'd
promised. And it wasn't a reason which she'd understand.
She did understand the vagaries of the kind of people who
are termed creative. Her father had been an actor of some
achievement before the alcohol broke down his brain cells

and her mother was a novelist whose work, according to the reviewers, was sharply observant, blazingly percipient, and astringently witty, but who as a person glided through life in a deep trance, making no contact at all with other human beings. Her brother Rory was an actor who seemed to be following in his father's footsteps, her brother Seamus was a poet who was mixed up with the IRA, substituting the gun for the bottle. Deirdre herself was a TV producer and – I expect in reaction to her family – was calm and practical and unfailingly competent.

She understood the vagaries of directors and script writers and actors just as she understood the vagaries of her family. But she wouldn't understand why I should break my promise to go to her country cottage with her simply because I wanted to think about Miranda. For she was in love with me and she wouldn't want to understand.

'Are you coming then, you bastard? I'm not asking you again.' In her anger her accent had intensified. It was normally very slight, less a matter of pronunciation than a lilt, an Irish country dance rhythm. Now it had a thick quality, was almost ugly. I wished that I could stop noticing such things.

I shook my head. 'I've work to do.'

'Do your bloody work then. But don't call me.'

She paused, scooping up her sunglasses and a packet of Sweet Afton cigarettes and her gold Dupont lighter from the bedside table. 'I'll call you. Like hell I will.'

She slammed the door as she went out; seconds later I heard another door slam, then the whir of a car starter, then the cough of an engine. The starter whirred again. I could visualize her pale furious face and her hand pushing the hair out of her eyes. She was stamping on the accelerator now; the engine roared. She didn't have a delicate touch with mechanical devices, though they

8

always functioned for her, as they never have done for me.

The Goblin Teasmade alarm rang and the kettle seemed to shake itself as if gathering up its energies. There was the sound of water pouring. I waited for five minutes to let the tea brew – mash I would have said once – and filled up a breakfast cup, barely colouring it with milk. The government health warning on the packet of Benson and Hedges on the tray was turned towards me: I turned it over and took out a cigarette. I've given up smoking more than once with the invariable result of eating more, and when you're only five foot seven an extra half-stone or so can make you appear absolutely globular.

Besides, I didn't believe that the only civilization in which I wanted to live would survive more than another ten years. I'd been thinking about that a great deal ever since my last visit to New York. There wasn't any sense in caring about what would happen to my body in my forties: it would be ridiculous to keep it healthy for the execution cellar or the prison camp. There's a terrible passage in *The Gladiators* where the prisoners awaiting crucifixion masturbate in order to wring the last possible pleasure out of their bodies and to weaken themselves and so make their end quicker. Personally I'd want to hang on to the last shreds of my dignity but the idea's a sound one.

I took the first swallow of tea. There's no drink quite so good, nothing to equal the first assuaging of thirst and the instant warmth in the stomach. And no cigarette to equal the first one. Since I decided some five years ago, not long after my divorce, that Western civilization was done for, I've taken an increasing pleasure in what are called the simpler things of life.

They aren't, of course, simple. It requires a power

station, a waterworks, and a complex system of distribution to bring one a cup of strong tea and a packet of cigarettes. A widespread enough strike, a few bombs, and there's no tea or cigarettes or power, water, light, heat or food either. There is nothing to be done about it when the people who run our society, irrespective of political party, so evidently desire its destruction.

There's a story about Stalin which has always haunted me. During the Great Purges one prisoner, despite all the horrors which were perpetrated upon him, refused to produce the required confession. Stalin asked the inquisitors how much the USSR and everything in it, with all its tanks, guns, aeroplanes, ships, soldiers and sailors and airmen, weighed. They said that the weight came within the astronomical realm, that it simply wasn't calculable. Stalin then asked how one man could withstand that astronomical weight and told them to bring the confession back.

And I cannot withstand the weight of the West's death-wish, cannot take on the mass media and the government and the law and the churches single-handed. And that is why I have no involvement in politics or public affairs: I'm determined to enjoy all that our civilization has to offer me up to the very end. Which means also that I write as I want to write – up to the very end. I don't have any illusions about what will happen to me. Having taken no part in politics won't save me. The elimination of all intellectuals – to use the word in its broadest sense – has been the automatic procedure whenever the enemy has taken over a country and there's no evidence that there'll be any exception in our case.

Those to be pitied are those who will welcome the enemy, may indeed have helped him, and who will be rewarded by being herded off with the rest of us. Even more to be pitied are those who will have a temporary usefulness, who may have a Zis limousine and a big office and special ration cards, only in the end to be declared enemies of the people in their turn, to be thrown away like used toilet paper.

I lie, and I had promised myself to be absolutely honest. Of course I don't pity them. My chief consolation before the bullet hits the back of my neck will be the thought that it'll be worse for them.

I briefly considered these facts – none the less facts for being in the future – before I turned my attention to Miranda. It was with a feeling of almost immoral self-indulgence that I did so. For in the process of explaining her character I have to explore my own. I have never been an autobiographical novelist; naturally I've always used material from my own life, but I've always been most economical with it. If you're not, if you transcribe your own experience direct with just enough alteration of names and events to avoid libel suits, then all too quickly you consume all your material, you're left with no alternative except to write about yourself writing.

And writing in itself is essentially dull – dull, that is, as a physical act. Or should I say, just for the pleasure of using the word properly for once, as a phenomenon? A novelist isn't like a surgeon or a soldier or an engineer, he doesn't, when he's working, inhabit the world where things happen: he sits alone making black marks on white paper. And the better a novelist he is the duller his personal life will be – not merely duller, either, but more and more non-existent.

That was what caused my divorce. Jean married a human being and found him changing into a phantom. The co-respondent wasn't her lover but my work. And my work was steadily disrupting our marriage long before she took her lover. That's one of the reasons why I don't feel bitter towards her. On my last visit to her she mentioned an old film she'd once seen, *I Married a Monster from Outer Space,* and started giggling. 'That's how I used to feel with you,' she said.

I fully comprehended her. And that is another reason why my novels have never, until now, been autobiographical. Novels ought to be about human beings, not monsters from outer space. I allow myself to write this novel now because in a sense it's not autobiographical. It's about Miranda Abberwick, whose novels were published under her maiden name Fewsey. I come into it incidentally, because our relationship is the most important part of the story.

We met in 1952 when I was eighteen and she was forty. I hadn't developed into a monster then and I'm not sure that she ever was one. Perhaps that was her problem.

I haven't seen her for three years, nor thought of her until the day before Deirdre walked out of my house. It took me six months and two affairs and some heavy drinking to get over my divorce, even though I wanted it and planned for it. But since then I've settled down to a novel a year with a three-month holiday between novels, working an office day from ten to six Monday to Friday and going out most evenings.

I knew that something was wrong when, halfway through a novel, I came to a dead stop. It's not an experience I've ever had before, except at the planning stage. Once I've planned a novel thoroughly I go straight ahead at a steady one thousand words a day. This isn't the only way to write a novel, but it's my way.

I was stuck for a full month and growing more and more worried. It wasn't money; if I never write again I'll have enough to keep me for the next ten years. It was not being able to write. If that left me, there was no justification for my keeping on living.

Then Miranda came up to the surface and I realized what I had to do. I believe now that she'd been there a long time and I'd been pushing her down because writing about her meant writing about myself and that meant learning about myself.

And that, I realized as I lay in bed drinking my tea and smoking, was the last thing I wanted to do. I know nothing about myself except the most obvious details – that my name is Tom Metfield, that I am thirty-eight years old, stand five feet seven, weigh nine stone, have fair hair and blue eyes and a fresh complexion and at certain angles have been told that I look like Jimmy Cagney. (This is odd, because if there's any Irish blood in my family I've never heard of it.) And I have an income in the region of £30,000 a year, and I now drink only moderately though I smoke more than I should.

I don't know much more about myself: I don't think that my likes and dislikes are very important. I've never found out very much from all the thousands of words which have been written about me, perhaps because most people confuse me with the heroes of my novels, particularly the first one.

I don't need to mention his name. It's sufficient to say that, unlike him, I'm not tall, I'm not handsome, I don't fuck everything that moves and I should be incompetent to earn any more than a bare living in the world of big business. I am quite simply and literally bemused and lost, an incurable neurotic with a knack of telling stories. I have no great gifts as a stylist but Alec Wallasley, one of my few friends, once told me that what he liked about my prose was that I wrote as I talked. I want no compliment higher than that.

And yet with every novel, imperceptibly, I reveal a little more of myself. And with every novel I destroy a little more of myself. The practice of any art destroys the personality as surely as playing the Jew's harp destroys the teeth. Perhaps this is why most artists today are Marxists; they hope that if the structure of society is reorganized, they'll become, to use the modish expression, fully integrated human beings. Before Marx they'd have hoped to be washed in the blood of the Lamb, the Lamb being not only Christ but rationalism or national independence or even parliamentary democracy. There are a lot more Lambs, but what it all boils down to is being beleaguered and expecting the United States Marines to come to the rescue.

But I have always known that blood is sticky smelly stuff which doesn't make one any cleaner and that the sound of the Marine bugle will be cut short by a bullet in the throat.

I shall not change. Unless disease or accident make my only reality physical pain. Or, worse still, transform me into a vegetable. I say worse still because then there's no way out unless, miraculously, there were a doctor or nurse with some compassion nearby.

But then of course I don't want to change. I'm happy with my life as it is. As I've said, I don't expect it to be allowed to continue: for two generations now those who lead the West have been offering its throat to be cut, and cut it will be. But until then I shall have had as full and happy a life as any human being can expect to have.

And Miranda is the one I have to thank. I might have made my way on my own but there was so much against me that I don't believe that I would have been strong enough. She gave me exactly the kind of help which I needed at exactly the time when I needed it.

And yet I resented her taking possession of my mind that August morning. I had wanted to go with Deirdre to Suffolk. I had wanted to continue working on my new novel.

The debt had to be paid: it was as simple as that. And there was only one way of paying it: to look back and see her as clearly as I could, and with love. I don't think that I have ever loved any other human being. I've spoken the words *I love you* often enough to women I've fancied, but the phrase has always been to me a password in a foreign language. One doesn't know what it means, but the sentries let one pass, and that's enough.

It's astounding how infallibly it has the desired effect. Age, experience, class, beliefs, make no difference. It's as potent with the militant decent members of Women's Lib, all aggression and unbound breasts, as it is with a starry-eyed little shopgirl waiting for Mr Right in her Maidenform bra. (Though one of the bonuses of the Permissive Society is that the password has been truncated; one isn't expected to add *and we'll be married till death do us part*.)

And yet I never have spoken those words to Miranda. The worst of it is that she would understand. She would understand even now. Am I frightened of her answer? Am I frightened that if she says *I love you too* then I shall begin to change? That I shall begin to love too many people, that I may, God help me, begin to love everybody, even those whom I would without a moment's hesitation have killed?

I don't even love my son Giles. I've never allowed myself to love him. I haven't seen him since his stepfather's job took the family to Scotland. My excuse was that at the age of two he'd soon forget me and that if I took full advantage of the rights of access there was a risk of

15

him growing up with divided loyalties. He seemed happy enough with his stepfather who, though he was without exception the biggest bore I'd ever met, was a kind and decent man. He also thought that Jean was wonderful and was naïve enough to continue believing in it. He loved Giles because he was Jean's son and the fact of him and Jean having a baby boy of their own would not make any difference. They were a family, and good luck to them. I owed it to Giles to let him forget me.

I made a very good short story of it a year after my last visit to Giles, naturally making all the necessary changes to names and circumstances and personalities. I don't often write short stories – as John Marquand said, they use up too many characters – but I fancied a girl who'd just gone to work at a trendy woman's magazine. Obtaining a contribution from me would increase her standing at the magazine and be the sort of gift which even the very rich young man who was currently pursuing her couldn't match. And I wanted to show that I could do it, that I could produce just the sort of stuff which they wanted, with credible characters and situations, but at the same time with a dash of the good old *kitsch*.

Most of all, though, I wanted to justify myself. In the story the hero resolves not to see the child again because he loves him so much and obviously he's going to keep on loving him.

I wish it were so: I might then be a better human being and a better writer. The fact is that I'm a coward. I can't bear suffering. I don't mean physical suffering for myself. I'll be absolutely honest: though I certainly don't enjoy it or welcome it, I'm better at bearing it than most people. It's partly due to my upbringing and partly due to my size. My father, who was a small man too, relished every moment in the Army, and was very proud of the bullet scar which ran down one side of his face. He taught me that the best way to avoid being bullied was to go in fighting. You still get beaten up, but eventually they choose easier prey. And he didn't have much sympathy for illness; he was never ill himself, and regarded all invalids as malingerers.

The result is that I can endure the sight of adults suffering with equanimity. I would just as soon not see it, but the thought of it doesn't come between me and my sleep. The vulnerable spot is children. Whenever I read in a newspaper of children dying by disease or accident or murder or of them being ill-treated in any way, I have to close my mind quickly. Even then my eyes prickle with tears.

There's an American medical novel by Morton Thompson called, I think, *No Man a Stranger*. It wasn't exactly great literature, but it was a competent professional job and it had an enormous documentary interest. I can't remember where and when I read it because I don't want to remember.

Let me get it over with. A mother has discovered her four-year-old son masturbating. She's furious and tells him that if he does it again she'll cut it off. She gives him and his little sister a bath and leaves the bathroom for a moment to get some soap.

When she returns he has a pair of scissors in his hand. 'Look, Mummy,' he says, 'I cut it off.' She screams and rushes out for help, not seeing his little sister falling back into the reddening water. When she returns the little girl is dead, the little boy dying.

I don't know whether I've got all the details right. I couldn't go back to the book again, even if I could find a copy. I shan't look at this passage again. There are moments when it returns to me and then I get drunk. I don't often get drunk, but it's either that or sleeping-pills. Did anything like it happen in real life? I asked a doctor once, and he told me that he'd known a similar case.

Jules Goncourt once said about God: 'Sometimes he strikes us as a terrifying torturer and executioner, a sort of superhuman Marquis de Sade. . . .'

That sums it up. But there's something worse that again I must get over with quickly, that again I can't bear to check. In any case, I gave the book, *Judgement in Jerusalem*, away as soon as I'd finished it.

When in an internment camp in France during the Occupation, Pierre Blum, the ex-Premier's brother, met a little Jewish boy. I think that the little boy was about ten, certainly no older, and his first name was Jacques.

Jacques, who was a bright and lively child, said that he lived in Paris and his father and mother were musicians. He would be seeing his mother soon, and he'd saved her a bit of bread from his supper.

Pierre Blum naturally could not bear to tell the child the truth. I don't know what he did tell him. Or what he could tell him.

The next day, if I've got it right, the child was still expecting his mother, still cheerful. The day after that, he wouldn't speak, was lost in grief, and there was nothing that Pierre Blum could say to console him. The next day he'd been taken off.

It's the child saving the bit of bread to give to his mother that always brings the tears. And I know that this story is true. I may have been inaccurate about some details, but that's because, again, I never wanted to remember it. I don't want to think of what went on in that child's mind. I don't want to think of the place to which he was taken off.

But when this story comes into my mind I feel only that I want to die. I don't feel guilty: that would be insane. How could I feel guilty, being only five when war broke out? But I don't want to belong to the human species. In Aloysha's speech in the graveyard at the end of *The Brothers Karamazov*, Dostoyevsky to me makes it plain that he doesn't intend to hand God back his entrance ticket. But I do, if ever I'm forced to think about it.

And that's why I'm resolved never to see Giles again. If he had only had me, it would have been a different matter. If he were in the least likely to be unhappy with his mother and stepfather, that would be a different matter; there are responsibilities which cannot be shirked.

But even in the normal course of things, even if the West hadn't signed its own death warrant, I couldn't bear to be a parent. When Giles was a baby I'd often wake up in the night imagining him the victim of every known calamity and disease. And, as other men have told me, that isn't the worst stage. The worst stage is when they become fully mobile and the dangers increase.

It isn't that I'm tender-hearted, though possibly I have a skin too few. It's that there's a limit to what I can take. And I'm not obliged to carry burdens beyond my capacity. I have built up a good life for myself. My work satisfies me completely. I live where I want in the sort of house which I want, furnished and decorated as I want. I'm not obliged to consider anyone else's tastes or opinions, much less their welfare.

And if I were obliged to, then my work would suffer. I put so much into it that there's little left over. I can't be simultaneously a husband and father and a novelist. I learned that during my marriage to Jean. And I also learned that there existed experiences which I couldn't live through and keep my mental equilibrium which, God knows, is tenuous at the best of times.

As it is, I have to be careful to shield myself from all the raw and bloody realities of life. The last road accident I saw – a ten-ton lorry had run over a Mini with a man, a woman, and two small children inside it – left me incapable of work for over a month. I came to the scene not long after it happened, and there was a small hand sticking out of the sleeve of an empty blue cardigan at least two hundred yards from where the lorry had stopped on top of the Mini. Yes, I used it, I couldn't waste it, but I would rather not have had it to use. Graham Greene has said that there's a splinter of ice in every writer's heart. And he's quite right; but without it their hearts would break.

I have to use whatever horror chance forces me to witness; but I don't go out of my way for it. It might have been different if my perforated eardrum hadn't kept me out of the Services, or even if my experience as a journalist had been less on the literary side. There are moments when I wonder if I shouldn't go to have a look at some war or disaster – it would be easy enough, either on my own account or for some paper, and there are always plenty of wars and disasters to choose from.

Perhaps it would make me a better writer, make me extend myself. It's more likely that I'd be unable to write again. And there's always the chance that I might be killed, which would be a shame when the Western world may have as much as ten years to go.

Giles is my Vietnam, my East Pakistan, my Aberfan. To love him, to love any child of my own, would be to take the risk of wrecking my whole life.

When I wrote down the story from the medical novel and the story of the little Jewish boy, I didn't go into the feelings of the parents. But there's another story, a true story, which keeps returning to me.

A nine-year-old boy had been sent home to die. He was in such pain that even the touch of his clothes was agony. His father had been told that he must save the pain-killing drugs the boy had been prescribed until the end was nearer, or else they'd lose their effectiveness. He couldn't endure to watch his son's sufferings any longer and smothered him. At the trial he was discharged absolutely. Some months later his wife left him and he hanged himself.

I don't know why the doctor couldn't give the child cumulatively increasing injections of morphine or why the hospital didn't. That's something else I don't want to think about. And a truly merciful judge would have had the father hanged. Our society is incomparably more humane than the society which will replace it, but I can't deny its streak of cold cruelty.

The story's about love, though. That's why it terrifies me. It was the kind of love that doesn't ask for anything for itself. Not even love back, and certainly, not even remotely, any kind of pleasure. And it consumed its giver.

I don't want to be consumed, but I want at least to come near the fringe of that sort of love, at least to begin to understand it.

And that's why, finishing my tea and lighting a second cigarette that Saturday morning, I looked back to the time when I was eighteen in a town on the Yorkshire coast. The strange thing was that as I settled down to remember Miranda there was a moment when the bedroom I'd taken so much pleasure in planning, with its cedar ceiling and red leather-covered walls and apricot wall-to-wall carpeting and curtains and huge double bed with a white coney bedspread that cost me a hundred and fifty, suddenly seemed intolerably bogus and stuffy, a *Playboy* reader's dream.

It's always been my pride to make myself absolutely clear, to drive the narrative forward with no jerks or clashing of gears.

But this is a rough road in a part of the world where I've never been before. All that matters is this bouncing and skidding, the springs creaking and the gearbox grinding, I've got through. Smoothness doesn't always matter. The truth always does.

Two

Engelsea is north of Scarborough, not very far from Robin Hood's Bay. The winter population's about 20,000, the summer population about 100,000. It isn't very keen on the summer population: the official guide uses the adjectives *quiet* and *select* rather a lot, and the Council rigidly limits the number of refreshment kiosks, beach vendors, trampolines, Punch-and-Judy shows, and the rest of it.

It started existence, like most seaside resorts, as a fishing village; most of the fishermen still live on the site of the original village in the Old Quarter east of the town. It would be agreeable to write glowingly of my boyhood by the sea and making friends with the fishermen's children and listening open-mouthed to some old salt's story of adventure as in the picture of Raleigh's boyhood.

But in fact I never talked to a fisherman in my life and the only old salt who was ever observed telling stories to children was eventually jailed for tampering with them. Nor did I mix at all with the fishermen's children; even at school they kept themselves to themselves. Not that I was encouraged to mix with them; they were a rough lot, and my father and stepmother were typical higher working-class. Or, to be more accurate, petite bourgeoisie;

my father ran an ironmonger's, later to become a Do-it-yourself shop, and my stepmother was the daughter of a café proprietor.

I never liked Engelsea very much and never felt at home there. I was actually born in Charbury in the West Riding; I was brought to live in Engelsea with my grandparents Knossington after my mother's death in 1942 from a totally unexpected heart attack.

I never felt at home in Charbury either. It's a large industrial city which used to have an abundance of Victorian buildings and which in consequence did have a surly individuality. Now it's been redeveloped and resembles Detroit without Detroit's crude energy. But even when it was still genuinely a place, my mother helped to put me off it. I was the reason for her marriage; my father, who had then acquired the first in a succession of second-hand cars, found himself and a friend in Engelsea one Sunday night in October and they picked up my mother and her friend Hetty Leagram. They had drinks – which my mother wasn't used to – at one of the first roadhouses to be built in the district; it was an unusually warm night for the time of year on the East Coast; my father was a good-looking young man with fair curly hair and (which counted a lot in those days) a car, and I was born almost exactly nine months afterwards.

I don't think that it was a very happy marriage. My mother never recovered from the shock of discovering that her lover was a joiner and that his father, mother, two brothers, two sisters, and all his relations without exception were, as she put it, as common as muck. And my uncle Cyril, the only one with any pretensions to gentility, had been to prison for receiving stolen goods.

My mother's father, Harold Knossington, owned two groceries, one in the west and one in the east end of the town. His father-in-law, Tim Rimswell, who was, like a lot of other people in Engelsea, related to the Knossingtons, owned two butchers' shops. With very few exceptions shopkeepers in Engelsea were either Knossingtons or connected in some way with the Knossingtons. And they had fingers in other pies too, notably land. Engelsea after the war became more and more residential in character; it had always been a popular place to retire to, but it was also convenient for the two new industrial estates which had been set up about fifteen miles north of the town. There were three Knossingtons and three blood relations of Knossingtons on the Engelsea Council, and somehow or other without any hint of corruption whatever changes came to the area benefited the Knossingtons. Some of them were to become very rich in a quiet, unostentatious sort of way: Knossingtons didn't flash their money around. And now the new generation of Knossingtons will no doubt enter the middle classes proper, become professional men and business executives.

And, paradoxically enough, would care far less if their daughters get into the family way by a joiner. In any case, there's always abortion. But that was then unthinkable. Apart from any other consideration the Knossingtons were Nonconformists almost to a man. My mother's parents – I can never without any effort think of them as my grandparents – had to make the best of it. They were just as pleased that my mother and father had a quiet registry office wedding in Charbury and that they wouldn't be shamed by the sight of my father coming home from work in his dirty overalls.

They never came to see us in Charbury, though my mother occasionally took me to see them. We didn't see much of my father's family either; most of them lived off Hurley Lane in the centre of the city and we lived in a cottage well off the tram route in Brylton, a dreary northern suburb. My mother didn't greatly encourage them either – except, surprisingly enough, my uncle Cyril, who always amused her and who, she said, had beautiful clothes and beautiful manners.

I've said that it wasn't a happy marriage, and so far it sounds like the conventional *Sons and Lovers* set-up – sensitive educated Mum, coarse primal Dad, super-sensitive son in the middle, all set to kill Dad and marry Mum. But it wasn't like that at all. Remembering being sent out to play one Sunday afternoon and coming back early with a cut hand and running round the cottage in panic to discover, finally, their bedroom door locked, I know that they were suited to each other in bed.

And it wasn't only that incident which makes me think this. I can remember looks between them, sly touches, even. I'll swear a suggestion of a smell, dark and musky, which used to cling to them some mornings. But we can't spend all our time in bed, more's the pity.

My mother was small and slim with large, brown eyes that were almost black, the colour of Bournville chocolate. Her hair, with a certain amount of help, was blonde. She read a lot, chiefly Mills and Boon's Light Romances. I don't remember any other books in the cottage, but I do remember a bright blue carpet in the living-room and a profusion of china ornaments.

I don't know why she wasn't happy with my father; my suspicion is that she was lonely. She considered herself several cuts above her working-class neighbours and the few middle-class residents of the village considered themselves several cuts above her. Looking back at Engelsea where she had high status and plenty of friends and relations, she saw it as the Great Good Place from which marriage had exiled her.

I was fed and clothed well enough but I don't think that there were many kisses and hugs. Frankly, I don't believe that she liked me very much. But there are no villains in my story: I was never ill-treated, merely left alone with my comics and plasticine and Dinky cars in a small room off the living-room which was originally called the Playroom and then became known as the Untidy Room.

Almost our only visitor from Engelsea was my mother's friend Hetty Leagram. Hetty was small and plump and red-haired and, at that time, inclined to fondle me a great deal. I can still recollect the disturbing sensation which the pressure of her soft but resilient breasts induced.

But one night coming out of the bathroom, I heard my mother's voice from downstairs. I hardly recognized it at first; it was raised high, screaming rather than shouting. I'd never heard her use that tone before.

'Go on, show him all you've got, you dirty whore! You fat, nasty, carroty bag! Pretending to be my friend, pushing your big tits in my child's face – '

There was the sound of a slap, and then my father's voice. I couldn't hear what he was saying. Then my mother screamed in earnest and for the first time I realized what it meant to have one's hair stand on end. A door slammed, and there was silence. Hetty didn't visit us again.

At that time Miranda was living in Chelsea and struggling to finish her third novel. She wasn't struggling in any other sense. There were a great many more newspapers and magazines then, and without much effort she was earning £500 a year (multiply by at least six to compare with present-day values). There was still a trickle of royalties from the first novel and she hadn't spent all the money from the film rights. She was an exceptionally good-looking woman when first I met her at the age of forty, but then she must have had the sort of face and figure which at first stir up desire and then take it a stage further. She was never really photogenic – her features were a hairsbreadth too bold for that – but looking at photos of her in 1939 and discounting the effect of the rigid waves of the black hair – dead black instead of soft black, with a tinge of chestnut – and the full mouth almost grotesque with lipstick like poster paint, one can see that she'd never have been short of escorts to wine and dine and lunch her and take her for long weekends in the country. She was still a name too. The man who was seen out with her would score twice over, he'd be ahead in the race, which is, at any rate amongst the rich, part of the fun of sex.

Her first novel, *Moving Through*, had been a solid success, with good reviews and a sale of 40,000. It's still in print. And there's been a successful remake of the film though she hasn't profited by it. It was considered very daring at the time: the heroine moved from affair to affair, from marriage to marriage, finally to accept the whole of life in the way that was fashionable before Hiroshima. Miranda could tell a story, she had some notion of how human beings behave, and she could write good plain prose. Over and above that, being a first novel, it had a certain coltish freshness, even its occasional clumsiness was endearing. Not that having said all that I'm any nearer the secret of its success.

'It can't be taken away from me,' she once said on a winter's night at the Coble Inn. 'Don't ever feel sorry for me. When you've made it, when you see people's faces change when they hear your name, it's as if – as if they were checking a hallmark. You're different, out of all those millions of people. And you're always going to be different. And to be *a name* in London – ' her eyes shone

– 'when you're young, to ride in triumph through Persepolis. You can go anywhere, you see, all doors open. For a while . . . But they *have* been open. And that was before TV . . .'

Her second book was received with little enthusiasm. She said that it was torn into small bleeding pieces, but this wasn't quite true. I looked up some of the reviews once and they didn't have the nastiness which they have today. It isn't that reviewers were fairer then, it's that publishers' advertising brought in more revenue. It would have been all the same whatever the reviews were like. The second novel was a flop. Honourably enough, she'd tried to do something entirely different, to take as her subject a group of men, to see them from the inside and women from the outside, and she'd bitten off more than she could chew. And there was no film sale.

She recovered – with surprising rapidity if what she told me was true. Of course, with her looks there were always plenty of men and not a few women around to assure her that the novel was far superior to *Moving Through* and that all reviewers were failed novelists and eaten up with envy and that true artists must always expect to suffer. . . .

So she got down to work on the third novel rather too quickly. That is, too quickly for her. In the light of what I know of her now, I believe that she should have gone out of London if not out of the country and devoted at least a month to thinking out what sort of a writer she was.

She didn't. She stayed in Chelsea and worked on the novel. The flat was in a street off Cheyne Walk and was all too convenient for her friends to drop in. It was all too handy for the PEN Club too, and she became involved in PEN affairs and, through people she met there, in politics.

There was nothing intrinsically wrong in this, and she was never a Communist nor even a member of the

Labour Party. It was wrong for her, though. She didn't have the ability to compartmentalize her mind, to allot her energies. Some writers can cope with both public life and private creation; she couldn't. It wasn't simply a matter of attending committee meetings of half a dozen different organizations; she contributed regularly to a now-forgotten magazine called *Warning*. Its aim was, of course, to warn the nation of the Nazi menace; it went through a confused period at the time of the Nazi-Soviet Pact and then after 1941 was taken over by the Communists.

As is the case with such magazines, it didn't pay its contributors. It paid its editor and its printers and its distributors, but the people without whom it couldn't have existed weren't supposed to need money. The money side of it can be discounted; one can always make more money. The irreparable loss is time.

'Don't ever write for nothing,' Miranda once told me. 'Not even when you're beginning. And never, never, never when you're a *name*.' She said *name* with a sad relish. 'If you've got anything worth saying or anything in the whole wide bloody world, someone'll pay you for it. And the public'll take a damned sight more notice of you in a national paper or magazine than in some crappy little amateur effort. Christ, how I used to sweat over those damned articles. Why did I do it? I didn't even enjoy sweating over them . . . Don't let me ever catch you doing that.'

She never did, and she never will. That's another reason for me being in her debt. I never have had any doubt as to how to plan my career. Scott Fitzgerald confessed to having been a poor caretaker of his talent; I have been a good caretaker of mine. I don't do anything unless I either enjoy it or am paid for it or consider it inescapably necessary. Since I resolved not to see Giles again there's nothing in my life which comes within the realm of duty, and all chores are dealt with by my secretary, my agent, my accountant, and my bank manager. All appeals for charity – in fact, all appeals for money for nothing – go straight into the waste-paper basket. And I don't answer questions about my work or give my opinion on unpublished manuscripts or open bazaars or address Speech Days or indeed talk in public at all. I've done an American lecture tour but I was well paid for that.

I don't have plenty of time, or even enough to do all that I really want to do. But thanks to Miranda I get by. I won't ever publish a novel like her third novel, about which I can only say that it wasn't the best she could have done. (I don't say that no novel of mine will ever be both an artistic and a commercial failure, only that I always shall have enough time to work with an undivided mind.)

It didn't get bad notices. It scarcely got any notices at all because by 1941 paper rationing had started and – perhaps it was the war, perhaps it would have happened in any case – Miranda was a name no longer. And there was no longer a living to be earned in free-lance journalism even if she'd not had the heart knocked out of her.

I know, piecing together odd things she told me about this stage in her life, that she drank quite heavily and slept around with anything in trousers if of commissioned rank and not, to use her expression, booksy. She didn't want to see any booksy people again and, by and large, it seemed that they didn't want to see her.

In 1941 she met Max Abberwick, a captain in the Duke of York's, who had then been seconded to the War Office. Max was a solicitor in civil life, a quiet, easy-going man some four inches above six foot, and broad with it. Miranda, being five foot seven in her stocking feet, had always preferred big men, and Max seemed kind, dependable and, being the head of a family firm of solicitors in civil life, would be well able to support her. And he wasn't booksy and didn't pretend to be: he cheerfully admitted to reading no books except the occasional thriller.

Miranda had had plenty of offers at the time of *Moving Through* but had in her head then the notion of dedicating herself to her art. She wanted her freedom. But now at the age of twenty-nine, with her money running out, freedom had lost its attraction. That attraction – and I don't blame her – had always been conditional upon success, upon remaining a *name*, or at least being able to earn a living from her writing. She could have got an office job easily enough – she'd done a secretarial course after leaving school. But after having been a professional writer for eight years – she'd given up her job at a publisher's when *Moving Through* had become a best-seller – she could not easily have settled down to working for anybody else. And at the BBC or the Ministry of Information she would meet the booksy people from whom she was now deliberately cutting herself off. And the Women's Services were unthinkable.

She could have gone home to Daddy, who was a vicar in a small village in north-east Surrey. He'd have taken her in as his bounden duty, but he and she had never been very close. Her novels, hard though it may be to credit it now, had shocked him; and, two of his sons serving in the Army and one in the RAF and his wife bedridden, he wouldn't have been easy to live with. He never was at the best of times. Miranda would have been treated as a prodigal returned but with no fatted calf; domestic help being virtually unobtainable even in that small village, she would have become an unpaid slavey. Worse still, everyone in the village would have regarded her as a failure, if only because at twenty-nine she hadn't got herself a husband.

So there was only Max. He proposed to her on the fifth week after their meeting. This was out of character; but he was forty, there was a war on, and he was the only son.

'He wanted an heir,' Miranda said to me. 'I suppose he was frightened that he might leave it too late. Well, he got what he wanted. Two heirs.' She laughed; it was a hoarse, rather masculine laugh. 'That was all that he *did* want, ducky.' That was in 1953, when we'd reached a startling intimacy, a greater intimacy than ever I'd reached with any human being before or since.

Or perhaps ever will again; I miss it still. I often wonder whether it didn't in some way cripple me. To be as near any other human being again would seem a kind of betrayal. I don't give myself to anyone, in bed least of all. I must have some affection and some respect for the woman I sleep with, and except for the period after my divorce, I'm literally incapable of a one-night stand. I don't think of women in terms of a quick roll in the hay, getting laid, getting my ashes hauled.

The first hero I ever created did think of women in those terms. He was a superb cocksman, ready and willing at any time. There are men like that; that's one of the things I learned from Miranda. You can only acquire reliable sexual information about men from women because whatever most men tell you about their sex lives is not to be trusted, even when they're drunk. And most men with the temperament of my first hero don't talk about it at all. Sex for a man is intermixed with pride and shame in a way which it isn't for a woman.

Naturally I made my first hero as unlike myself as possible. I couldn't have written about him otherwise, because I knew virtually nothing about Tom Metfield.

Without Miranda my first novel would have had far less impact. I wouldn't have begun it with an extra ration of experience, and the best kind of experience, which is other people's. The heroine of my first novel is based on Miranda. Max, as she said, married her because he wanted an heir, and that was all that he did want. Had he wanted more than that, it's possible that I shouldn't have ended up as Miranda's confidant, her beloved companion.

Beloved companion? I look at the phrase again, and must let it stand. I was more than a friend and more than a lover. The insertion of my penis into her vagina (not that I never had dreams of it) wouldn't have deepened our relationship but have brought an element of unreality into it. I wouldn't have been able to see her as she really was, she'd have taken me on a path along which any other woman could have taken me. And that would have been a waste, because what she gave me no other person at that time and place could have given me.

And yet I've found myself wondering if it wouldn't have been better if she'd become my mistress. There are rules which it's best not to break. The Gods of the Copy-Book Headings – though mine, I dare say, are other than Kipling's – shouldn't be disregarded. There are healthy and unhealthy relationships. Miranda gave me a head's start in my career. She gave me a love which was to sustain me through the years ahead, which still does sustain me. It sustained me when I didn't realize it. But it was a bit too much like the love that God is supposed to have for us all. And that's too near for comfort: I was and am her creation.

Perhaps I'm now trying to retrieve the balance, make her my creation instead. Perhaps I'm making a bid at freedom, if I want that kind of freedom. Perhaps I should try to be a well-adjusted personality, as the Americans are fond of saying. And I can only begin to be well-adjusted, to have meaningful relationships, to be integrated, by shaking myself loose of Miranda, by firmly categorizing our relationship as unwholesome and starting to think about her in that light.

The light of the reading lamp on the psychiatrist's wise, kindly face, the patient looking at him adoringly from the darkness – no, it won't do for me. I don't want to be well-adjusted or integrated, and I'm never quite certain exactly what constitutes a meaningful relationship. What I am certain about is that now I'm as happy as any human being can expect to be and that if I hadn't met Miranda I'd now be existing in a state of growing frustration, a teacher or provincial journalist at the very best, but more likely an alcoholic or drug addict. It just isn't true that talent will out, though it's a comfortingly cosy belief.

Miranda moved to Abberwick Grange, Max's home, as soon as she was pregnant. That would be in the autumn of 1941. Abberwick Grange was a large eighteenth-century house in local stone standing on a plateau within sight of the sea. The Abberwicks had originally been yeomen farmers and had owned most of the land in Engelsea. The Grange had been built by an Abberwick who had too great a fondness for brandy, cards, and horses, and the family fortunes weren't restored until the mid-nineteenth century by Maximilian Abberwick, who was something of a recluse, drank only tea and much preferred making money to spending it. When he'd made enough, however, he started entertaining lavishly, took his place in County society, and got married, rather late in life, as all the Abberwick men tended to do. (Or so his namesake once told me.)

Max's mother, who in 1942 was tall, energetic, tweedy,

and more County than the County, was living at the Grange; she liked Miranda partly because of her looks but more, I suspect, because Miranda came of what is known as a *good* family. The help that couldn't be got in the South could be got in the North, and Mrs Abberwick would in any case have been quite capable of looking after Miranda single-handed.

Miranda was glad to be out of the battle. The days were filled by her children and long walks and reading and day-dreaming and visiting and being visited by the few people in the district whom Mrs Abberwick found socially accept-able. She ate well – fish was plentiful and the Abberwicks also had farmer relations.

The wounds inflicted by the failure of the third novel began to heal. After the birth of her second son she made several attempts to start a fourth novel. 'But there never seemed to be time, darling,' she told me later. 'So I gave up. I told myself that I was saying goodbye to literature, living my art. I was doing a Rimbaud – one was a very comfortable Rimbaud, of course . . .'

Max went to France in 1944 and didn't come home until 1946 during the Nuremberg trials. Mrs Abberwick died in 1947, and with her death Miranda felt that her Rimbaud period had ended. The wound had now com-pletely healed and she could always tell herself that the third novel had been a casualty of the war. And Max insisted upon the children having a Nanny as he himself once had, and the haphazard wartime domestic help was replaced by a man and wife as general handyman and resident housekeeper. Miranda now had far more time and began to make notes for her fourth novel. But when I met her she'd ceased even to make notes.

In 1942 my mother died of a heart attack. My father was in a training camp in the West Country at the time.

And here I come across a difficulty. I've already used her death and can't describe it again half as well. I've even used our kitchen where she died one November morning, falling forward across the big scrubbed pine table and breaking her nose in the process. I remember the crunch of breaking bone and the scream cut short by a whistling sound which was a minute later mimicked by the whistling kettle on the gas stove. There was a little blood from her nose, but only a little.

My father came home on compassionate leave and then went off to the Far East. And I went to live with my grandparents in Engelsea. I wasn't very happy there, but that part of my life has no place in this story. My father was demobbed in 1945 and on his return to England promptly married Hetty, who had been married and divorced to a Canadian airman during the war and had a three-year-old son.

They were both in the same boat of course; they needed to get married again, and wouldn't find the right partner easy to come by. Over and above all this, to be quite fair, I believe that they had a genuine passion for each other. At the age of eleven, I didn't see things in quite this way: Hetty to me was a wicked woman who, God knows why, I was convinced was responsible for my mother's death.

I kept this all to myself, but it was the main reason for my failing my eleven-plus. Hetty had a daughter some ten months after marrying my father and that didn't make things any better. Now my father was involved in the death of my mother too. And my grandparents both resented him taking me away from them and his marrying Hetty. They had only brought me into their home out of a sense of duty in the first place, but it's possible they might have grown fond of me or at any rate used to having me about the place. And the Leagrams they thought of

37

as being rather low, and non-chapelgoing into the bargain.

I can sympathize with all the parties concerned now. My father – and I don't blame him – wanted to get married and settled down. He was a healthy man of thirty-four and had been a long time without a woman. And he had, as I've said, a genuine physical passion for Hetty. My grandparents, on the other hand, cared chiefly for their standing in the shopkeeping Nonconformist community. They wanted, as they themselves would put it, to be able to hold their heads high in Engelsea.

Their life was one of hard unremitting work, of steady accumulation of safe investments on earth and of grace in Heaven through good works and regular chapelgoing. It wouldn't be my life-style and young though I was, I knew it; but I wouldn't be a novelist if I couldn't see how firmly and contentedly they were committed to it.

I'm not yet ready to write about my schooldays; I liked neither my elementary school nor the secondary modern school (as they were called then) which I entered at eleven and left at fifteen. I didn't do very well at the latter; the headmaster was very keen on the handicrafts side and I've never been much good with my hands. I was quiet and morose with few friends and appeared to my teachers slow-witted to the point of being moronic. I enjoyed reading anything I could get hold of, but kept quiet about it; neither my father nor Hetty approved of the habit, possibly because it reminded them too much of my mother.

I wasn't ill-treated either at home or at school. I was left alone to sort out my problems, which I summarize by the statement that the physical world is highly complex and cannot be described except perfunctorily in abstract terms. The grey stone school high above the grey sea, my father's grey terrace house near the shop, my father's shop with the rows of wood and stacks of paint tins and all the tools and gadgets each one of which he knew the function – how could a few words locate and identify them, much less celebrate them?

But it wasn't until I was fifteen and was working in my father's shop that I began to see that my function was to celebrate. Began to see very dimly, but with great urgency; there was something which I had to do in connection with the actual tangible world around me, and that was writing.

It would be wrong to say that I was unhappy. It would be wrong to say that I was happy. I had found out what I wanted to do; and with fierce energy I set out to do it. I wrote a good deal – generally a story a week – and it was all rejected. For until I met Miranda I simply didn't know how to set about it.

Three

Miranda didn't look her age; there was no grey in her hair
and she had no need of corsets. I knew this because black
hair is the most difficult to touch up, never being pure
black but having a red or a blue tinge; and with the best
corsets in the world, no matter what the advertisements
claim, there's always the tell-tale outline under the
clothes, always some point where there's a slight bulge,
always stiffness where there should be springiness. She
didn't come into our shop; she wasn't the do-it-yourself
type. But I saw her frequently walking along the Front
with her Old English Sheepdog Hemingway, so named
because he was large and strong and clever and had a lot
of hair.

Sometimes I saw her at the County Library branch, a
converted shop on the Promenade, about three hundred
yards from my father's shop. The Front ran parallel with
the Promenade Gardens, with a wide stretch of turf and
flowerbeds between them. At the fishermen's main quarter
it narrowed into Main Street and branched off into the
Filey Road. Miranda always walked along the Front and
then into the fishermen's quarter from where she'd take
a footpath across the fields from the Filey Road to the

Grange. She always wore brightly coloured clothes regardless of whatever the fashion might be – scarlet and blue and gold and, above all, white; and she never seemed to be seen twice in the same outfit. When she was in the library at the same time as me I always contrived to move near her because I liked her smell so much. I didn't know much about perfume then, but my nose told me that her perfume had an ambergris or civet base and that the soap she used wouldn't be bought at the corner grocery.

I didn't think of her in sexual terms. She was, for one thing, tall for a woman and, unlike many small men, I'm not turned on by tall women. And she didn't have a good complexion; the heavy powder couldn't hide its orange-peel texture. Her age, too, put me off. I am not, I repeat, the hero of my first novel. Naturally I wondered from time to time what she looked like beneath her clothes, but only briefly and ashamedly. The notion of making love to a woman of forty seemed to me then vaguely incestuous: I honestly felt that at forty sex stopped.

I had known that Miranda was a novelist ever since I'd come to Engelsea but the knowledge didn't register until I read *Moving Through*. I can still enjoy the book now, with all its faults, but its effect on me at sixteen was explosive. At that time no writer could go into too explicit detail or use four-letter words; the majority either cut at the crucial moment or used some very fancy metaphors, like Hemingway with the earth moving for Robert Jordan and Maria. The trouble with this method is that the reader can't always be sure of just what happened and that sex, even a sixteen-year-old virgin in Engelsea is aware, just isn't like that. Cutting is preferable, though it introduces an invisible censor and cheats the reader.

Miranda, mostly by the proper use of dialogue, showed the reader the act itself. It wasn't merely a question of what was said during the act, but afterwards in other places than bed. Love does have a language of its own – there are times when the cliché is unavoidable – and messages in this language delivered in the drawing-room and the office are like a shot of Polish vodka in cambric tea. You either have the ear for it or you haven't. Miranda had it, so she could write about love; and she could write about death too. (Being a parson's daughter had probably given her an edge over most writers.) And that is what all art is about.

My literary guide at first was my cousin, Maurice Knossington, who was a trainee teacher. Maurice had gold-rimmed spectacles, very blond, almost white hair, and a round rosy face; he had a cheerful disposition and a kind heart, and a habit of always telling the truth which could sometimes make him uncomfortable company. He had – and it's rarer than is supposed – a genuine love of books. Being able to talk about books with him rid me of some of my isolation.

But he was a devout Methodist, for which (mistakenly, I think now) I rather despised him; and he was always trying to persuade me to take my Matric so that I too could become a teacher or a librarian. I couldn't bear the idea of teaching and though I liked the branch library at Engelsea with its smell of books and Pollywog paste and floor polish, I didn't like the rows of issue tickets behind the counter nor the stacks of membership forms, overdue notices, and the rest of it. The books were one thing and the machinery for issuing and recording them was another. Learning to write was one thing; studying for Matric was another. I knew even then that there wasn't much time and that there never would be. But Maurice meant well; he himself had found his vocation and he thought that I was in danger of missing mine.

One night in early 1952, as exactly as I can place it – it was a clear moonlight night but as bitterly cold as it only can be on the East Coast – Maurice and I had gone to the branch library together. Miranda had just left with a book on interior decoration and her perfume still lingered. It was the smell of London, of wild girls who resisted you tooth and nail and then turned soft, it was Chelsea, it was Soho, it was films and TV and publishers' contracts, it was freedom and in amongst it was me, a different me, a Name as Miranda would have put it and indeed as I myself put it then. Miranda had published three books. Miranda was even now part of that world. Miranda was in *Who's Who* and mentioned in several books on the novel; I would live out my whole life and it would be as if I had never existed.

'It's a long time since her third novel,' Maurice said.

The librarian looked at her wrist-watch and the clock; we hastily gave her our books and went out onto the Promenade.

We both wore duffle coats, supposedly ex-Navy surplus, which were fashionable at the time. I put my hood up, holding it down at the neck; the perforated eardrum which kept me out of the Forces had been giving me trouble, and a piercing cold wind had just sprung up. As cold as a stepmother's breath, I said to myself, as cold as a witch's tits; there was a man from Northumberland who came into the shop who used the phrase *a sour blow*. It was exactly right when he said it, but it wouldn't do for narrative, because of the association of blow with fisticuffs. The Promenade looked desolate in the moonlight, half the shops darkened; through the duffle hood the swishing of the waves was transmuted into a rhythmic grunt. I had seen it many times before and each time it was different; I knew that it had to be remembered because it deserved remembering, because there was no-one else who could or would remember it. And simultaneously I hated it, wanted to be in the London of *Moving Through*, of cafés and pubs and clubs and restaurants and all-night delicatessens, of the crowded streets and blazing lights, of Soho and Chelsea, of Nina Hammett and John Gainsworth and Jack Benney and Ironfoot Jack and James Agate of the Café Royal and the Café An, of the Wheatsheaf and Fitzroy and the Marquis of Granby – of a Soho and Chelsea, though I didn't know it, which were already disappearing. There had been a literary London, there had been a Bohemian London at the time that *Moving Through* was published; but even as I dreamed of it in Engelsea it was ceasing to exist. The reason was quite simply rising London property values: Bohemia is of its essence where Bohemians live, it must be near the publishers and newspaper offices and art galleries where they can earn a living, and the rents must be low. I didn't then know these economic facts of life. But I don't think that the dream did me any harm, and it helped to sustain me through the rejection-slip period which was under my circumstances inevitable. There were the cold moments of depression when I could foresee myself still working at my father's shop in Engelsea thirty years ahead; they came and went as they had done in the library, but I never had any lasting doubts of my vocation and my destiny.

And as I walked along the Promenade with Maurice, I had already the idea for a story. There was some special quality of Engelsea that moonlight night that set my imagination to work. Walking past the lifeboat station in the fishermen's quarter I was seized by the fact that all these buildings had been here long before I was born and would be here long after I was dead. It wasn't an original thought – even I at the age of eighteen could see that – but if I looked and listened and smelled, if I

44

gave the thought to someone who was usually untroubled by thought of any kind, then I would have something original, because I would perceive Engelsea at that unique moment in a way that no-one else could perceive it.

At that date Main Street was still lit by gas lamps painted green, with fluted columns and crossbars with spikes on top of the lamps. On a dark night the gaslight had an orange tinge; tonight it was a pale yellow. The shopkeepers in the Promenade kept their windows lighted after closing time and their signs were inclined towards the modern; here the windows were unlit, except for the chemist's, and the signs were mostly wooden in old-fashioned lettering. In a niche over the chemist's door was a large iron mortar and pestle. Main Street was winding and rose to the north; it was tarmac, like the narrow side-streets which ran off it, but in my story I decided to put down cobblestones.

The fishermen's quarter wasn't in fact really picturesque, though the narrow streets with their alleys and courtyards did have a certain charm. There were a few old cottages nearby; they weren't owned by fishermen but by retired people. Virtually all the buildings in the fishermen's quarter had been built in the 1850s by one of my ancestors, Martin Knossington, who had, uncharacteristically for a Knossington, lost most of his profits in speculation.

The terrace houses were of local stone with no attempt at any kind of ornamentation. They looked solid enough; I didn't know what they were like inside because I didn't know anyone in that part of the town. For the story I gave them stone porches and tiny front gardens and put the date 1850 above the top house of the street I was looking at. I changed the name, Elizabeth Street, to Clipper Street, and kept the lifeboat station and slipway at the bottom of it.

45

My hero was six feet tall with a thin, slightly dissipated face. He was thirty, which at that time seemed an interesting age to be. The problem was what he should do for a living. I decided to make him a successful shopkeeper, shopkeeping being the only occupation I knew much about. He would be married with a plump young wife and children; like my cousin George Knossington, who was the jolliest of the family. I had to try to see *inside* George, who was certainly untroubled by thought.

'It's darned cold,' Maurice said. (He never swore; a rather irritating habit.) 'If you're dreaming up a story, dream it up on the move.' I followed him down Main Street, looking up most of the time at the moonlit sky, trying to find some image that would sum up that enormous uncaring expanse of bleakness; it had to be an image which would occur naturally to George Knossington.

We turned to the right where the Coble Inn stood in a small square with the seawall at the bottom and two shops and a café, closed down for the winter, at the left. Going into the Coble Inn I suddenly realized that I didn't relish trying to see inside George Knossington, that he was indeed the jolliest of the Knossingtons, but that he was also the most earthbound. He thought my ambition to be a writer a great joke, and addressed me habitually as Dopey or the Hermit and, in masculine company, would jocularly accuse me of wanking myself to death. 'It's all these dirty books he reads,' he'd say. 'It'll turn you blind, Dopey. You won't be able to do anything with a woman when you get one . . .'

I wasn't such a fool as to allow myself to be seriously perturbed by him, but I had to pass George Knossington and Son, Est. 1900, Gents Outfitters, every day, and though I varied the time he always seemed to know exactly when I'd pass by, and would emerge from the interior of the

46

shop to pass in his loud hectoring voice (as if always calling a meeting to order) comments upon masturbation, day-dreaming, the length of my hair, and my choice of shirts and ties.

Ordering two pints of bitter in the Lounge Bar, a small oak-panelled room off the main Lounge, I discovered that when I pursued the idea of George as a character in a story, liking or not liking him ceased to be relevant.

'Good for what ails you,' said Maurice, taking his first mouthful of bitter. He was one of those people who needed alcohol to brighten him up; I am one of those who need it to calm me down.

'I'm surprised at a good Methodist like you saying that,' I said. A liking for beer was Maurice's sole departure from Nonconformist orthodoxy.

'No harm in any of the gifts of God if used in modera-tion,' he said.

'To hell with moderation. And God doesn't give us any-thing. We take what we want from the old bastard.'

I always enjoyed shocking Maurice; I have an unreason-able feeling of guilt about this now.

'He loves us,' Maurice said. 'He gives us whatever we need.'

'I need something right now,' I said. 'I need to see my-self in print.'

'You could pray for it.'

I laughed theatrically. 'Maurice, you'll be the death of me. Do you think He cares?'

'If He sees the fall of each sparrow – '

'Bullshit! Anyway, all that means is that He *sees* it. It gives Him a kick, like seeing babies shoved into the incinerators does.'

The rest of the argument doesn't matter. We'd had it before. At one moment I could believe that he was wrong and at another that he was right. At that moment it seemed to me that to accept a set of beliefs which acknowledged what I had just felt looking at the moonlit sky was more mature than simply to reject, using, what was worse, my father's arguments ('It stands to reason, doesn't it? If you'd seen what I'd seen at Tobruk . . . *Merciful* God! Bugger that for a tale . . .'). I didn't have to become a Methodist. But I did have to acknowledge the mystery all around me, not only in the moonlit sky but in the blazing fire in the grate in the Lounge Parlour, in the murmur of voices from behind the frosted glass partition to the right, in the dark green of the sea through the windows to the left; and the search for the correct image for the sky meant merely that I was too intellectually snobbish to accept the terms which Maurice and the millions like Maurice would accept.

We'd finished with religion and gone on to argue about *Ulysses* when Miranda entered. There is in most places one pub into which an unaccompanied woman may go without being taken for a prostitute. The reason for this is generally that it's used by a reasonably respectable group of men and women. Miranda's Gang were this group. I don't know why they chose the Coble. It wasn't particularly old – mid-nineteenth century – it looked like a barracks, and the interior was rather gloomy and nondescript. Tourists went to the Lord Cochrane, a late eighteenth-century pub with thick walls, mullioned windows, and a lot of rather good ship prints and ship models and nautical bric-à-brac.

A few fishermen used the Lord Cochrane, but most used the Coble, though not the part we were in. They preferred the taproom with its wooden benches and sanded floor. It had a separate entrance and an outside urinal; it would have been possible to have used the pub every night of your life and never to have met a fisherman.

Not that this worried Miranda, any more than it worried me or, for that matter, the fishermen. She was not one of those intellectuals who take a great delight in meeting the People (so unaffected, so downright, so earthy, so refreshingly *real*) and sharing their simple pleasures of darts and dominoes and shove-ha'penny without a hint of patronage (fatal, my dear, they're very *proud*) just as if they were members of the People themselves. Miranda never even pretended to like any of the People, nor did any of her Gang.

Strangely enough, I didn't until that evening know about the existence of the Gang. (Miranda, half-facetiously, had called the group the Souls in the beginning, but the Gang was the name that had stuck.) So I was surprised to see Miranda by herself, saw her for a moment as a sexual being. Miranda ordered a whisky and dry ginger, lit a cigarette from a gold case, looked at us coolly (we were actually trespassers, this being the Gang's room) but gave Maurice a half-nod. She took out a copy of the *New Statesman* from her large black shoulder-bag and began to read, but she hadn't got very far before Ralph Thoralby and Ted Lewis came in.

They kissed Miranda effusively, both, I thought, making rather a meal of it. I noticed when they took off their duffle-coats that they were wearing clothes like mine – coloured shirts, woollen ties, tweed jackets, flannels in the case of Ted and blue corduroys in the case of Ralph. This was at that time the intellectual's uniform, together with brown (always brown) brogues, occasionally in suède. Polo-neck sweaters and crew-neck sweaters were sometimes worn, but always in heavy wool for warmth. Only Colin Wilson, some two years later, wore polo-neck sweaters all the year round. And hair, for those days, was worn long – which is to say short at the back and sides but when combed down falling well over the eyes.

What is extraordinary, looking back, is the uniformity of ensemble. An intellectual – to use the term in its broadest possible sense to cover artists and would-be artists – instinctively, wherever he lived, however isolated he might be, wore this uniform. Maurice wore a tweed jacket and flannels and brown brogues, it is true. But his hair was short, and his shirt was white with a separate collar and his tie was patterned rayon. And he had a white handkerchief in his breast pocket, folded into two symmetrical triangles. Display handkerchiefs were not worn by the Gang; Ralph had a red Paisley handkerchief stuffed loosely into his breast pocket, which was permissible, since he used it to clean his spectacles with and it didn't even faintly match his tie or shirt.

I have made a great deal of this because it was important to me. As soon as I saw how Ralph and Ted were dressed I knew that they were my kind of people. I would have been sure of this if they hadn't said a word, even if Ralph hadn't in a voice calculated to carry over to my corner referred to *dear old Kingsley*. He meant by this that he personally knew the editor of the *New Statesman*. (And indeed, though I didn't know it then, he once had had a piece of reportage published by the *New Statesman* during the war.)

To say that something is difficult to describe is a laziness I rarely permit myself. But it is difficult to describe what I felt that evening in the Coble; perhaps only those who have been through the same isolation will understand. I did have some confused notion in my head about loneliness being essential for the artist; but in practice it's a wretched state.

As I eavesdropped upon Miranda and Ralph and Ted,

I'd never felt happier in my life. For I could pick up all their allusions. I wore the correct uniform, and, above all, I was a writer. Not a published one, but I was going to be published. My instincts told me that on that very night when I'd looked at Main Street and at the sky above I'd taken the right direction.

Another man and a girl joined Miranda's party. The girl was plump and pale in a belted coat which did nothing for her figure, but her face framed in the scarlet babushka was interesting, with large brown eyes and a full mouth. Here surely was a genuine wild girl – she had a bundle of magazines and papers, including the *New Statesman*, under her arm as if to prove it – with whom one could make love naked in the sun, who would scorn the bourgeois bondage of marriage, who might even write herself. Who might even write about me: One winter's night in a little town besides the North Sea I met the love – and the bane – of my life, the man with whom I was to spend five stormy years in Paris, Madrid, and Provence; the man who was to wreck three of my marriages, the man who after all these years I cannot think of without an exasperated tenderness and – shamelessly an old woman confesses it – a helpless lust. When we met at the Coble Inn that night he didn't speak to me, merely looked at me. He walked across the room to me, small but incredibly lithe, compact, energy-packed, dangerous; a silence fell over the room and he took me firmly by the arm and out of the room. It was as if my companion didn't exist. Not until hours later, drugged with pleasure, naked in his arms (I was rather vague as to where this would happen, but hoped that she would have a place of her own) did it occur to me to ask his name. 'Tom Metfield,' he said. 'You've never heard it before. But one day everyone will hear it. And this night – it won't be wasted, it will be remembered all over the world . . .'

Her name was Jane Badingham; like so many in Miranda's Gang, she was a teacher. The young man with her, Harvey Abington, was a WEA lecturer. His subject was literature and he had already had a few reviews and articles published, and was now contemplating a novel. He was engaged to Jane; I noticed her ring just after I'd taken her to bed. He was tall and had a slight limp, the result of – in his own phrase – a lump of shrapnel he'd picked up in Normandy. I bitterly envied him this, even more than I envied his possession of Jane and his publications and his height and his clipped officer's accent and his enormous fluency.

Maurice and I continued to argue about James Joyce but my heart wasn't in it. I wanted to be over in the Gang's corner; they now had got on to the subject of Marxism. I noted a strange similarity about the men's faces: they were all inclined to be sallow with long faces and their hair was lank. Ted would be about twenty-one, Harvey twenty-eight, and Ralph forty; it was as if they were the same man at different ages.

'Marx explains it all,' Harvey was saying. 'Intelligence, morals, religious beliefs, oh, everything human, are determined by one's economic environment. You, Miranda, are the product of a corrupt bourgeois society. Which isn't to say that you're inferior in any way. On the contrary, you're superior. The exploitation by your ancestors of the proletariat has given you good teeth, strong bones, firm flesh, and a lively intelligence. Your husband has continued exploitation on your behalf . . .'

'Darling boy,' Miranda said, and patted his hand. 'I've heard it all before, my poppet. And really – ' she had a husky drawl, modelled, I imagine, on Kay Hammond's – 'I've never exploited anyone in my life. I've been exploited by bloody publishers, editors, agents, the bloody lot. And the film bastards – '

'Of course. You are both exploited and exploiter. Sexually too.'

She smiled. 'Oh, I don't mind that, darling. But I don't agree with you. A fuck is a fuck is a fuck.'

I don't think that I'd ever heard any woman use that word casually before. It gave me a sharp thrill and an immediate erection; but the erection wasn't connected with Miranda. I could grasp the fact of her sexuality just as I could across the room smell her perfume. I could sense the tensions between her and the three men, I could sense Jane's slight jealousy; but I didn't myself desire her. An obvious way to put it would be that I felt towards her as a son to his mother, and the obvious way would be correct.

'Did you hear that?' Maurice whispered, obviously shocked. 'And she's supposed to be a lady – '

'She's the product of her economic environment,' I said.

'Of course, *Moving Through*' – he was still speaking in a whisper – 'was nearly banned. The library still gets complaints about it.'

'Do you know anything about Marx?'

'Doesn't everybody?'

'I don't.'

'I'll lend you a book about it.'

'You tell me. I haven't time. I've a story to write.' I had decided that I'd call it *1850, Night, Moon, Sea*; it was already taking shape in my mind.

'Everything in the universe is material. There is no God. That's a bourgeois concept to enslave the proletariat. There is no after-life, only this life . . .'

'Seems pretty sound to me.'

'It doesn't to me, but never mind.'

'You needn't explain that you don't believe it. Go on.'

He went on.

He was well-read and had a retentive memory and, which doesn't always go with it, the ability to render down to the essential. When he had finished I knew as much as I would need to know about dialectical materialism, the class war, economic determinism, surplus value, alienation and the root of it; what I have learned since has all been founded on that. And I had found the almost laughably simple answer to whatever questions I might have asked myself about God. It was enough for me then.

We left Miranda's Gang still arguing at a quarter to ten; Maurice had reached his limit of four pints and I wanted to begin my story.

As I left him at the top of Orkney Street, the terrace where I lived, he said to me: 'Why don't you send some of your stuff to Mrs Abberwick?'

'It's such an *amateur* thing to do. She won't read it.'

'She will if it's any good.'

'How do you know?'

'I don't think anyone thinks of her as a writer much any more. That lot she was with are too interested in themselves.'

'I didn't realize you were listening so hard.'

'You're not the only one who listens.' He smiled, which he didn't do very often. 'But say a lot about her work,' he added with unexpected shrewdness. 'She'll help you. If you're any good. Like Flaubert and Maupassant.'

'Oh hell. I don't like to – '

'No need to swear, old man. I think your stuff's not bad, but I'm not a writer, am I?'

'I'll think about it,' I said.

But a fortnight later, having had the story typed by an agency, I posted it to Miranda.

Four

Maurice had been right; no-one was taking much notice of Miranda as a writer at this time. *Moving Through* stayed in print and brought in a steady trickle of royalties; but no-one seemed to write to her any more. Fan-letters (an awful phrase, but what other is there that fits?) are a time-consuming nuisance just as requests for interviews and talks and opening Speech Days are, but as long as the flow is continuing, a writer is sure that he's making connection. Once the flow stops, he's alone in the void. I'd taken special pains in my letter to say much more about Miranda's work than my own, to make the enclosure of my story seem an after thought.

It was a fortnight before I had any answer from Miranda and during that fortnight I grew increasingly nervous, making more and more mistakes at the shop, hardly able to keep my temper with my stepbrother Lester (named after his Canadian father), and unable to settle down to either reading or writing. My chief consolation was my half-sister Amelia. Lester was horrible, large for his age – he'd be ten that year – and rather fat. He didn't like me and I didn't like him; but my father did, because he was always getting into fights which invariably – or so he said – he won.

The house at Orkney Street had only three bedrooms and I shared a bedroom with Lester. This meant that I couldn't read or write in bed with any degree of comfort, and that I had to keep all my manuscripts locked away. Lester was both inquisitive and destructive; he once tore several manuscripts of mine into shreds and then put them into the dustbin. My stepmother did reprove him but only mildly; she, like my father, couldn't really understand all the fuss about a few bits of paper.

I learned to write when Lester was there in the other bed, bribing him with sweets to keep quiet. I even learned to write in the crowded living-room with the whole family there and the television going full blast. The television was my father's and Hetty's favourite toy, partly because few people in Engelsea at that time owned one. It wasn't easy to work with it in the background, but I didn't have much option, the bedrooms being totally unheated. The bonus has been that ever since I've been able to write anywhere; I rather despise the sort of writer who can't work except in comfort and seclusion.

But I wouldn't like to go through those days again; it took extra energy to divide my attention between work and messages from the outside (Tom, fetch the coal in, there's a good lad. What are you writing, Tom? Tom, do you hear me, fetch the bloody coal in. Tom, what do you want for your supper?) some of which could be disregarded and some of which had to be received and acknowledged and acted upon.

I retreated from the battle, sitting staring at the television with Amelia on my knee, taking her for walks, telling her stories. I was happy in a way, even though I knew that I was wasting time, that if I were ever to become a professional writer I must write every day regardless of what I felt.

56

Amelia was small for her age, with skinny legs and arms, fair hair, and a thoughtful expression. She was far from being weak and sickly, a Victorian angel child; she ailed far less than Lester, and was far less faddy an eater. If only misuse hadn't given the word sweet the taste of saccharin instead of the taste of wild honey, I'd call her sweet. But the word is past redemption now, so I'll say simply that she was gentle and loving.

Sitting in the cluttered living-room in front of a roaring fire looking at the TV I'd stop thinking for hours on end. My stepmother didn't have particularly good taste; the shabby brown cottage suite, the orange wallpaper with its pattern of roses, the bulbous shiny sideboard, the bright blue carpet, and the Victorian mahogany dining-table didn't exactly add up into a harmonious whole. Yet the room had an atmosphere of warmth and comfort I've never found anywhere else.

My father and stepmother went out most evenings in the shop van. Lester generally played out till bedtime. My father and stepmother seemed to go out more than usual that fortnight; I could have done a great deal of writing, since if Amelia saw that I was working she was quite happy to play on the floor with her dolls, talking to them in a low soothing voice. But I was waiting for Miranda's verdict: I had made my mind up to abide by it, whatever it was.

If I wasn't a writer then I had to acquire some kind of qualification before it was too late, before I got past sustained mental effort. I didn't relish becoming a teacher or a librarian, but it was better than being a not very efficient shop assistant.

I don't think that my father minded one way or another. He wasn't an ambitious man himself and didn't have any ambitions on my behalf. Nor did he have any desire to found a shopkeeping dynasty. He made a fair living from his shop then (and now with the influx of new residents from the industrial estate at Engelsea he has a detached house outside the town and a Volvo shooting brake to replace the Ford van). But basically, like most working-class people, he lived for his leisure: the shop was for him a way of earning a living, not a vocation. And he and my stepmother remained physically obsessed with each other: they were husband and wife before they were father and mother.

This isn't to say that they neglected their children or had no affection for them, merely that they had no plans for them. Neither of them was in the least frustrated, they didn't have any need to live through their children. I'm now inclined to be grateful for this; there were moments in my youth when I should have welcomed some intelligent interest but never at the cost of being emotionally smothered.

During the fortnight of waiting for Miranda's verdict I don't suppose that I've ever been more desperately nerve-wracked. Since then I've had longer periods of waiting for other people's decisions but as you grow older you grow more resilient, you realize that no failure must be accepted as final. And yet during that fortnight I was nearer to being a full member of the human race than ever I have been since.

For I loved and was loved, and it was the simplest kind of love, asking for nothing for itself. Amelia was a very restful, composed little girl, who didn't talk very much and who had the gift of physical tranquillity. My father and stepmother described her with accuracy as being old-fashioned; she was always neat and didn't like to get dirty. Before her bedtime she would ask for a story. 'Not a sad one,' she would say. She couldn't bear to think of anyone suffering, even the Big Bad Wolf. So instead of being boiled alive he jumped out of the pot, ran away, and became a reformed character.

After the story we would have tea and biscuits – cambric tea for her – and I'd brush her teeth and put her to bed. Sometimes she said she was frightened and I'd stay with her in the chilly little bedroom until she went to sleep.

Whatever I have written about parent and child has been founded upon my relationship with her. Naturally I've drawn upon my own experiences as a father, such as they were, and I've observed the few parents I've met together with their children. But what knowledge I have of what a father feels for his child has been based upon my recollection of what I felt for Amelia. And sometimes I hate myself for this. I wish that I didn't have to *use* everything. It's as if she'd saved up her Saturday penny for a present for me and I'd sold it for a pint of bitter. I thought at the time that I was loving another human being, that and nothing else: but I was mentally taking notes, I was going to *use* the experience.

What I feel for Miranda is different. She was – still is – the same kind of person as me. Loving her doesn't preclude my analysing that love. And my using the experience doesn't devalue it. The emotion remains the same whatever I do with it. That's why it's the only genuine love I've ever felt for any other human being. I can't be sure about Deirdre or any other women I've ever slept with. I only know that after Eros has been given his head, what one feels begins to change. Eros only keeps up the pace over the short distance. Perhaps the orthodox moralists are right and it takes ten years of marriage before one begins to love a woman. But I can't make the investment in time and effort. I'm not interested in anything so expensively speculative. I must make do with Miranda, about whom I'm sure, who'll ask for nothing I can't give and who never did.

I got her letter one wet Monday morning in early March. It was in a deep blue envelope, addressed in rather dashing but obviously feminine handwriting. It smelled of sandalwood; the rather melancholy odour, brought out by the rain, cut through the smell of the breakfast bacon and black pudding.

My father's nose twitched. 'Birds writing to you now.' He mimicked a female voice. 'Dear Tom, you are the father of my child . . . Come on, let's have a look.'

'Leave the boy alone,' my stepmother said.

'It's from a – friend. About a story of mine.'

'Oh, we know those stories. It's all lovey-dovey will you marry me until you get what you want. And you only eighteen, you dirty bugger.'

'That's a rude word,' Amelia said. 'You're not to say that word. And you're not to say horrid things to my Tom. How you dare!'

'Oh, you stick up for your brother, don't you? I just hope he's been a good boy.'

I don't think that he really cared. Nor did I mind his banter very much. I knew that neither he nor my step-mother would insist upon knowing what was in the letter, any more than either of them would have opened it.

'She wants to talk to me about my story,' I said. 'She thinks that it has definite promise.'

'Who's she?'

'Mrs Abberwick.'

'By God, *I'd* better start writing stories. She's more in my age-group anyway. And her husband's getting on . . . You'll learn a lot from her, lad.'

My stepmother frowned. 'Don't talk daft, Ken. It's very

kind of her to take an interest. Everyone's not like you, sex-mad.'

He leaned over and pinched her bottom. 'I know someone else who's sex-mad,' he said. She giggled.

I find it pleasant to remember that morning now. I was beginning to admire my father for his swaggering gamecock masculinity and I had long since passed the stage of blaming him for my mother's death. And I thought of my stepmother as Amelia's mother rather than as a stranger who had replaced my mother. I had my spasms of curiosity about what went on between her and my father in bed, and now and again I would find myself looking at her legs or her breasts too searchingly. But I didn't allow myself to think of her in a sexual way; not for reasons of morality but of self-preservation. My father would literally have killed me if he'd suspected I'd even thought of her physically. And she was always careful about how she sat (which wasn't difficult in the skirts of those days) and how she dressed about the house.

Perhaps this is why Miranda's letter, though almost intolerably exciting, and looked at again and again, didn't hold for me the promise of any sexual delights. *I've been rather under the weather for the past fortnight, which is one of the reasons why your very kind and perceptive remarks cheered me so greatly. I would very much like to talk to you about your story, which seems to me to have enormous promise. But between promise and achievement there's a great gap, which perhaps I can help you to narrow. Please 'phone me and we'll discuss it here —*

So I was lucky. It's not a pretty thought, but had my mother been alive, her attitude towards my going to see Miranda would have been very different. Somehow or other it would have been spoiled, I would have been made self-conscious about it. And if my mother had been alive

I would in any case have had less freedom than I had. I don't think she would have been the smothering kind, simply that her interest in me, even if intermittent, would naturally have been more intense than Hetty's. I find it pleasant to remember that morning because at a crucial stage in my life I was left alone.

I remember it with pleasure; but there's always something to pay. I was never quite as close to Amelia again because I didn't need her quite as much. We still loved each other and I am still, nearly twenty years after, a better person for that love. I don't think that she felt hurt or rejected and, after all, she had her parents and her friends were beginning to be more important to her. But the high point had been passed.

There is nothing to be done about it except to be grateful. I have had more than most men have and I have missed much of what most men have. But at least I have had the love of a child at its purest.

And let that stand. It exactly defines what I mean, and I won't revise it in conformity with the prudery of our age, the weird prudery out of Marx by Freud which either detects a sexual element in all kinds of love or stigmatizes love which isn't sexual as sentimental and unreal.

I 'phoned Miranda that morning and went to Abberwick Grange that evening at nine o'clock. That was an adventure in itself. Unlike my first hero I had no romantic vision of one day living in a house just like the Grange; my feelings as I walked up the long winding drive were those of a biologist discovering a new species, a chemist discovering a new formula – they were professional and in a sense impersonal.

The drive was bordered with shrubs, mostly laurel, dark green and glistening with the rain: the drive was newly laid with tarmac, which showed up light grey against the dark shrubs. From the Filey Road I could hear the occasional sound of a car and in the distance the murmur of the sea. The rain had stopped, leaving a huge stillness behind it.

There was a hard tennis court in front of the house and a lawn of about two acres behind it with rock borders. The house was plain, even severe in its outline, with short windows on the ground floor and taller windows on the first floor and a pillared front door big enough to drive a horse and carriage through. There was a carriage lamp on either side of the door; those were the only jarring notes. They were too quaint, they were too picturesque, they didn't belong; whoever had designed that house would no more have used them there than we would today use motor-car headlights. There was a courtyard to the right with a wrought-iron gate which didn't belong either – again it was too quaint, too picturesque.

It did of course occur to me as I stood looking at the house that it represented a good deal of money, that simply to keep it in its present sleek, well-cared-for condition one would need £1,000 a year at the roughest of estimates. And £1,000 a year then was a good income.

But these calculations were done rapidly. What was important was the sense of having begun to change my life there under the new moon. I should be seeing a lot of big houses all over the world. I should be making many journeys. And I was always going to be alone. I sniffed the smell of grass and earth and wood brought out by the rain; a breeze sprang up bringing with it the smell of the sea.

I pushed the faintly glowing doorbell button. It seemed a long time before Miranda opened the door in an ankle-length fluffy white housecoat.

'I'm sorry,' she said. 'The housekeeper's off – her bloody

old mother's ill, selfish old bitch. And Max has had to go to London. Do come in, darling.'

She took my coat and tossed it on a wooden chest in the entrance hall.

'I was asleep,' she said. 'It's this wonder drug the doctor's given me. I'm his guinea-pig, you know.'

The dark blue fitted carpet felt very thick under my feet. The house was very warm. At that time I'd not been inside a private house with central heating; it seemed the height of luxury to me.

Miranda smiled. 'You don't really like that shade of blue, do you? Or that awful yellow zig-zag pattern.'

'It doesn't go with the house,' I said.

'You're right, ducky. It's very good carpet: Max got it during the war in a moment of madness. But I'll make him change it sooner or later.'

She opened a door off the hall and showed me into a small room with white and gold striped wallpaper and a large white Indian carpet. There was a low table with a tray of bottles and glasses on its black marble top.

'Help yourself to a drink,' she said. 'I'll have a very large Scotch.' She went over to the small desk in the corner. 'Here's your story. And my comments. We'll go through it if you can bear it. Can you bear it?'

'It's very good of you to take the trouble.'

'My dear, it's the first time ever that anyone sent me a manuscript with the faintest *glimmer* of talent. Close your eyes.'

I closed them, puzzled. Then I remembered the scene from *Moving Through*. I would open them and she would be naked. To my horror and bewilderment the prospect saddened me.

'Now describe this room.'

I described it down to the black basalt fireplace and the

electric fire with one bar switched on and the half-dozen small military miniatures on the wall opposite the door.

'I can't describe each uniform,' I said.

'Describe the sofa.'

'Sort of Grecian. Gold brocade.'

'It's genuine Regency. More comfortable than it looks. You've done very well. Open your eyes now.'

To my relief she was still wearing the housecoat. She saw me looking at it.

'Pyrenean wool,' she said. 'Very comforting. I can't get warm today.' She lay down on the sofa. 'Don't look so apprehensive. I'm not going to die on you. And do pour the drinks. There's a box of cigarettes on the table.'

I poured the whisky. The glasses were very heavy crystal.

'Get yourself a little table and be comfortable,' she said. 'And bring me one.' She took her gold case out. 'These are very strong,' she said. 'But you can have one if you like. Sure?'

I shook my head and took a Passing Cloud from the silver cigarette box. I was feeling a little sick with apprehension.

'The title,' she said. 'It won't do. Too clever-clever. I've made some suggestions. And your hero – he's absolutely unreal. I mean, I think it's jolly good making him a rather crass shopkeeper and not an actor or a painter or even, God help us, a sensitive young writer. But I can't believe in him.'

'He's a real person,' I said.

'No, love. He's too much of a piece, too consistent. There never was anyone like that.'

'I see what you mean.' I didn't see what she meant.

'It doesn't matter if he's said the exact words in the story. It doesn't matter if you *know* the story happened to him. It doesn't matter if he looks exactly like the chap in the story. What matters is whether the *reader* feels he's a real person.'

She looked smaller in her housecoat and together with her scent there was the smell of sleep; as she shifted position slightly on her sofa it occurred to me that one simple movement would bare her loins. If she'd had it in her mind to seduce me, that would have been the time. And then my first novel would have been very different.

But what made me banish the notion of sex from my mind was the profound intoxication of having my work analysed by someone who knew what writing was about. The problem of the writer learning his craft is the lack of expert appraisal. I had enough commonsense to know that it couldn't be bought, that those who offer to teach or rewrite upon payment are as seedy and crooked as those who sell infallible betting and pools tips. But those who know how to write, my instincts told me, haven't the time to tell anyone else.

So I knew the value of what I was getting. Already, though, I had the intimation that I was getting something else – the beginning of friendship, the experience of being treated as an equal by a much older person. Sex didn't matter in comparison with that. So I kept my eyes on her face and asked: 'Shouldn't I use real people, then?'

'Just their exteriors. A bit here, a bit there – not all of them all at once. And things they say, if they're interesting or shocking or funny or sad. And bits of what happens to them. It's no use, you see, if you don't make it your own. But don't worry too much about people now. It's *things* which count. I don't give a fuck – ' I thought that she darted a glance at me to see whether this shocked me, but I may be mistaken – 'for the people in this story. What's good, what's true, is the description of this miserable little town out of season, on a cold night. You've noticed things

66

I've never noticed, like the pestle and mortar outside the chemist's. It's a good start . . . But you're a bit of a mystery, aren't you, my dear? I mean, I don't know much about you, except what's in the story.'

'There's nothing about me in the story,' I said.

'Oh yes there is,' she said, and inhaled deeply. I noticed that the cigarette was a Capstan Full Strength, not generally thought of as being a woman's cigarette. 'You'll get used to that. You strip yourself every time you put pen to paper.' She smiled indulgently. 'I know you're a virgin, for example. Aren't you?'

'I'm not – not quite. I've had some experience . . .'

'Not as much as you'd like. It's just as well. Repression doesn't do as much harm as they say. Of course, I can tell a lot of things about you now. You're not really a drinker; you've forgotten your drink. A real drinker would have had two by this time, even at eighteen. I'm glad about that. And you like women, which isn't always good. If you get married too soon, you'll be finished as a writer.' She fell silent for a moment. 'I think it's finished me. Not any-one's fault but my own . . . But tell me about yourself. From the beginning.'

I told her as briefly as I could. I wanted her to keep on talking about the story.

'Extraordinary,' she said when I'd finished. 'So much for all that bloody nonsense about economic determinism. You're not politically-minded, are you?'

'It's too boring. And there isn't the time.'

'Better and better. Then you won't waste any of your time as I did. But you'll have to be careful. The day's coming when you'll have to make obeisance to all the correct causes before you get a decent review. Which will mean all the Left-Wing causes. You don't understand me now, but one day you will.'

This was extremely far-sighted of her, that being a period when the cultural Establishment was basically conservative. To me then it meant nothing.

'You mean I must say what I don't believe?'

'No. Just don't get mixed up in politics. Politics ruins more writers than drink.'

It was pleasant to be called a writer by a writer, but I was growing impatient. I had come to talk about my story.

'Do you think anyone'll publish my story?'

'No, dear. But you might get an encouraging little note on the rejection slip if you hit upon an editor who isn't a clapped-out old hack. There just isn't much market for that kind of story anyway. I could tell you how to write the kind of story there *is* a market for, and even now I think you could bring it off. But that isn't enough for you.'

'You mean it's no good,' I said, a little sulkily.

'You wouldn't be here now if I thought that. I want you to rewrite it, but not as a story. Just keep in the descriptive stuff. Don't muck about with it – just write as if you were seeing the place.'

'But that wouldn't be a story.'

'The point of the exercise, love, is not to write a story but to get published. I know where a piece of reportage of the proper length is pretty sure to get published – particularly since you're eighteen and it's about the North. The industrial North would be even better, of course . . . Have you a copy of the story? Good. Chuck it over then. Look – ' she beckoned me over. 'Cut here and here and here. Give me a pen from the desk. Now. Cuts here and here and here – ' the pen slashed – 'and sharpen it up here. Dream up at least two original images.' She saw the expression of doubt on my face. 'Yes, you can. You can do anything when you have to. Begin with a bang and end with a bang. Write a bit over a thousand words –

you've plenty of leeway. Always leave something to cut. The editor's a false-faced heartless old bastard but he's not a bad judge . . .'

I walked home half-delighted and half-frightened and wholly exhausted. It was the first time that I'd ever encountered a genuinely powerful adult personality, its edges hardened by early success and the cut-and-thrust of metropolitan literary life, and with the self-assurance of wealth behind it. There was something else too, though I didn't see it then: a growing bitterness, a growing frustration. She intended to pummel me into shape to make her way back from exile; I would deliver a message from her which would have to be listened to.

It was only about two miles home down the Filey Road, up Main Street and into the Promenade and Orkney Street, but it seemed interminable. Filey Road was a long straight road bordered by fields; there were no hills, no landmarks, no houses to relieve the eye from the all-reaching flatness. Trudging along the wet road I had the fear of being lost, of going the wrong way to Filey; it was a fear entirely without foundation, but it added to my fatigue. I think, too, that I was frightened of not being able to rewrite the story, of being rejected by Miranda; I told myself that I couldn't possibly sharpen it up, dream up two original images, begin with a bang and end with a bang. She treated me altogether too much like a professional, I couldn't cope with it. And I wasn't going to spoil a good story.

But entering my father's house I knew that I was going to rewrite the story in the way Miranda had suggested. My fatigue was intensified by this knowledge; I greeted my father and stepmother briefly and sat down in my usual chair to look at the manuscript.

'He looks thoughtful,' my father said from behind his

paper. 'Well, they say that lady writers keep it in the same place . . .'

'She gave me a lot of good advice.'

My stepmother handed me a cup of tea and sniffed.

'And some whisky too.'

'I only had one drink.'

She laughed. 'Better be careful then. Your father might be right about older women.'

'I'm always bloody well right,' my father said.

There was a scuffling noise from behind the door and Amelia entered in her pink dressing-gown, her feet bare.

'I can't go to sleep,' she said. She came over and sat on my knee; I put the manuscript in my pocket.

This generally happened about once every two weeks: normally I didn't mind, but I could have done without it tonight.

'It's late,' I said. 'Why don't you just go back to bed?'

'You take me, nice old Tom.'

'Mummy'll take you.'

She shook her head and tightened her arms around my neck. Her cheek was very smooth and the small thin body felt warm through the dressing-gown.

My stepmother smiled. 'It's you she wants, Tom. She thinks the sun shines out of you.'

My stepmother had her faults, but jealousy was not amongst them. And perhaps she had the idea that Amelia's affection for me took the curse off her being my stepmother. If this was what she felt, she was right, but I wouldn't at that moment have objected to Amelia being taken away from me. I wanted badly to look at the manuscript, not actually to work on it but to daydream about it. And then there came a sudden warm love for the child; perhaps I realized how little of that kind of love I would receive in the future.

70

'Say goodnight to Mummy and Daddy then,' I said. I took her over to them and she kissed them; then I carried her upstairs. Her room was small and chilly but it was newly decorated with a pink nursery wallpaper with fairies and pixies, the dressing-table and bed and wardrobe and chest-of-drawers were a new and expensive suite in white, and there was deep pink and white fitted carpet, which was more than there was in the other bedrooms. Her dolls were in a neat row on top of the white toy-chest; there was a large rather scruffy once-white doll in the bed, a cross between a teddy-bear and a rabbit, which she called the Snow Baby.

'Cuddle me,' she said.

I knelt down and cradled her head with my arm.

'Go to sleep now, love,' I said.

'Tell me a story.'

I told her the story of the troll and the three Billy-Goats Gruff, having the troll run away back to the troll's country and settling down there with a lady troll and becoming a good kind gentle citizen. At the end she closed her eyes and slid down on the pillow; I waited five minutes then took my arm away. She opened her eyes again. 'Stay with me.'

'Go to sleep, pet.'

'Stay with me a little bit; I do love you.'

'I love you too.'

I set down the words as they were spoken. I had heard them before and was to hear them again; but that night they nearly made me cry.

I had a sudden apprehension of what it was like to be a child, of how much in the world of the child large warm comforting presences were needed, just as it was needed to make small manageable worlds, the worlds of the doll's house and the doll's tea-party. There was another world outside the circle of the nightlight on the dressing-table, large and cold and mysterious with no dolls or cuddles or cambric tea; I held her till she went to sleep, then very gently took away my arm.

When I went downstairs my stepmother smiled at me and went into the kitchen. She reappeared as I was going through the manuscript and put down a tray of beef sandwiches and a pot of tea on the table.

'We're off to bed,' she said. 'Lock up, Tom.' She smiled at me again. 'Don't stay up too late.' She looked at my father. 'Come on, let the lad get on with his work.'

She didn't generally bother to make me anything at this time of night, and she and my father generally preferred me to go to bed before them.

'You're a good boy,' she said as she left the room. My father said nothing, but he ruffled my hair as he passed, something which he rarely did.

The fire was low now but still bright. I let the tea stand for five minutes then stirred it. I took the first gulp and felt its warmth down to the pit of my stomach. Then I turned my attention to the manuscript again. Her writing was very easy to read, and the paper smelled faintly of her scent.

Five

Rewriting the story was more difficult than I'd anticipated. What did Miranda mean by sharpen, smooth, cut, point up contrast, establish subsidiary theme here, and where was I to find original images? And naturally I resented throwing out the story, which occupied roughly two-thirds of the piece.

I had had the experience of rewriting before too, when the editor of a little review, long since defunct, had suggested that I revise a story and had returned the revised version with a note to say that I'd somehow lost the freshness and bite which I'd shown before. (It gave me great pleasure to meet him at a publisher's party years later, now a boozy hack on a trade paper.)

But I worked hard on the piece, querying every word and, whenever I was in doubt as to what Miranda's suggestions meant, put in an original image. And I took the same walk again twice, in solitude, to get the details right. I didn't see Maurice, and I kept away from the Coble. It wasn't easy, because up to then I'd worked in bursts and revised very little – I believed in inspiration, in being absolutely spontaneous. And, being eighteen and a virgin, my mind was for most of my working hours – and in my dreams too – steamed up with sex. I could put sex into stories; I couldn't put it into a straightforward piece of description.

And yet I believe that it was there all the more strongly for it being repressed. It wasn't that I used sexual imagery, that I looked at Engelsea as if the place were a woman; it was that my approach was sensual, not intellectual, that I concentrated upon the actual with a passionate exactitude.

I realized on those two solitary walks that I wouldn't stay in Engelsea all my life. I had to extract all that I could from it since no other place would ever mean so much to me again. I would never be entirely free of it, it would enter into everything that I wrote. There would be many other solitary walks, that would be the recurring image of my life. These walks – or rather this walk – along the Promenade and Main Street would set the pattern for them all, the lights in the windows of the little houses would be all the lights that would never shine for me. I would always be on the outside.

Not that this was an unhappy period: I was beginning to realize what my vocation was. I have only been un-happy since then when I've tried to evade the obliga-tions of my vocation, tried to live as if I were an ordinary human being. I don't mean that a writer is superior to non-writers; in fact, in most ways he's decidedly inferior. I wouldn't want any child of mine either to be a writer or to be married to a writer. I've known a great many writers; I've never known one who wasn't deeply flawed as a human being. The few who were anything like decent human beings weren't very good writers. And my friends among writers – and perhaps my only friends are writers – have never been those. I couldn't be friendly with an incompetent writer because my awareness of his incom-petence would always come between us.

More and more strongly as I grow older I'd like to be stronger, warmer, gentler, more loving, to be able to respect my friends for something more than their talent. I have no friends to whom I could go for moral or spiritual help and guidance, not one who is any better than myself. Of course, I spend more time in bewailing this than in doing anything constructive about it. When I was eighteen it was enough that I wasn't lost and despairing any longer, as I had been until I left school. From the date of that first meeting with Miranda my happiness began.

I don't mean that I can't be hurt, that I'm immune to misfortune and disaster, that I don't often wish that there were something outside my vocation in which I could immerse myself, whether a personal relationship or politics or religion. I don't mean that there aren't days, sometimes weeks, when I'm seized by emptiness, an absolute conviction of futility.

Not then, though. I finished the piece and sent it to Miranda and almost by return post had her answer.

Meet me tomorrow at the Coble – at 7. I think something can be done with this.

That was all; it was enough to irradiate the rest of the day with a wild joyfulness. I rushed through my tea that evening and was in the Lounge Parlour of the Coble at half-past six, half-an-hour before Miranda was due. I was wearing my usual weekday brown Harris tweed jacket, but I'd put on a new pair of brown corduroys and a new shirt in dark green and a new woollen tie in a lighter green. The water hadn't been hot enough for a bath, but I'd washed my feet and changed my socks and underwear. I had even had a shave, the second that day, which I didn't really need, and which had left my face tight and smarting.

It was a wet cold evening but that was precisely the sort of weather which at that time I enjoyed and still do.

I had a good Denbyrane trenchcoat of the type that was fashionable then, and my shoes were Lotus Veldtschoen. I didn't have a very large wardrobe, but what I had was good, partly because I could get clothing at a discount but mostly because my father had a horror of the cheap and shoddy. I expect that this was a characteristic of a generation which had grown up before the notion of planned obsolescence occurred. It was also a characteristic of someone who lived in the physical world, who as a workman and a shopkeeper was vitally concerned with the physical qualities of things.

It is important to note what I wore that evening; whether we like it or not, we live in the physical world, our thoughts are shaped by the objects around us. We were still then in the pre-plastic, pre-synthetic, pre-frozen food and disposable container era; virtually all artefacts were solid, a little clumsy, and made to last. I waste no time deploring the inevitable passing of this era but I am its product – heavy, a little archaic, not very easy to handle but, I hope, solid and durable.

And so I sat, solid and durable in my solid and durable clothes, waiting for Miranda in the Lounge Parlour of the Coble. I was smoking Capstan Full Strength because I wanted to be able to give Miranda a cigarette and to prove that I had noticed what she smoked; the combination of the cigarette and the local bitter made me slightly but agreeably dizzy. The fire was burning brightly and the room was very warm after my walk through the rain.

There was no-one else in the room. I was glad of the chance to get to know it. The bench seats against the walls were covered with beige Rexine and the padding was lumpy, the chairs were covered in the same material, the fitted carpet was in an ugly dark brown shade like the curtains, and was nearly piebald, and the tables were iron

76

with a great deal of scrollwork on the legs, which bashed many a shin and ruined many a pair of stockings. The oak panelling had been stained a dark brown and tobacco smoke had given the ceiling a yellow tinge; the best feature of the room was the large stone fireplace in the wall next to the Gang's corner; but even that seemed as if made for a bigger room.

And yet there has been no room which has meant so much to me, in which I have lived so intensely. I sat and dreamed there until Miranda came in, wearing a bright red raincoat and bright blue slacks and kissed me on the cheek, a gesture which at that time and place and at my age I found enormously sophisticated.

'I thought we'd have a quiet word, before the Gang come in,' she said, taking off her raincoat with a flourish. The barman, a tall, thin middle-aged man, with Marcelled blond hair, silently put down a glass of whisky. I fumbled in my pocket, but she pushed my hand away. 'No, no, my poppet. Rule Three of the Gang: we pay for our own shorts.'

'Thanks ever so,' the barman said. He left a smell of eau-de-cologne behind him. I sniffed; this was in the days before after-shave for the masses.

'He's a sweet man,' Miranda said. 'Who are we to judge, et cetera? Well, my dear Tom, I've been burning up the 'phone today, running up a most *tremendous* bill, and finally I settled upon Jack Royston, who was the chap I had in mind anyway. He's a Grade A bastard – he lived with me once and the things I could tell you about him – but he runs a good magazine. And he loves giving the proles a chance. So, my chickadee, your little piece is in the post.'

'You didn't have to alter it?'

'Only the *tiniest* scrap here and there. You really are a natural, you know. Of course – ' she was now not looking at me at all – 'sometimes it's just a freak. There's just this one thing someone can do – '

'I can do anything,' I said fiercely. 'You'll see. I've got lots of ideas – '

'Don't be so fierce, honey. Of course you have. I was merely thinking aloud. Very naughty of me.'

'That's – like what you do on the piano – '

'Five-finger exercises.' She smiled. She had very good teeth.

'Five-finger exercises. I'm going to write stories. And novels. And plays.'

'In good time, my pet. In good time.' She patted my hand; her hand was very cool. 'I've been thinking a lot about you. You've so much to learn, and there's never enough time. Oh Christ, no!' Her mouth contracted, the faint lines on her face for a second deepened. 'No. Time runs away from you. And then it's gone. It's not original, darling, but I had a lot of time once – oodles of it, stacks of it. And then – where the hell has it all gone? God only knows. Do you ever think about God? Do you?'

'Not often.'

'But you'll die, you know. My brother died, and he was only twenty. Do you think you can't die?' There was a rather aggressive note in her voice.

'I just don't think about it. Not for myself.'

'Of course not, darling.' She rapped her glass on the table. 'Not at your age.' She accepted a cigarette from me, then arched her eyebrows. They were heavy, but finely modelled. 'You noticed. That's splendid. When you're older, you'll realize how little things like that count with a woman. Do you know, if I ask my husband to get me cigarettes, he never knows what kind to get me?'

There didn't seem any answer to this, but I mumbled something.

'Well,' she said, '*à nos moutons.* Our plan of campaign . . .'

But she didn't have the chance to get any further because at that moment Ralph Thoralby came into the room. He frowned for a moment when he saw me, then smiled.

'So you're the young genius I've been hearing about,' he said. He sat down, rather heavily.

Miranda seemed rather put out by his entry. She introduced us and then excused herself.

'Marvellous woman,' Ralph said. 'You're very lucky. She'll teach you a lot about writing. Actually, it's what she needs. She's going through a very bad patch . . . She needs something to occupy her mind . . .'

I wasn't very pleased at being regarded as a sort of good cause, a way of helping Miranda; it must have showed on my face because he added hastily: 'She wouldn't bother if she didn't think you had real talent. She's a damned good judge.'

Miranda came back into the room and said rather coldly to Ralph: 'You're early.'

He seemed embarrassed. 'Something came up.'

'I don't give a fuck.'

'I could tell you if – '

He gestured at me.

'No. Have a drink. It'll keep.' She gave us one of her brilliant smiles and started to talk about Katherine Hepburn. I don't know why she didn't continue to talk about her plans for me, or else take Ralph apart to discover what was on his mind; but the subject was still films when Ted Lewis came in, and then others of the Gang; that evening I didn't talk much, but there wasn't any need to. My first publication was imminent, and, almost as important, I was now on the verge of joining Miranda's Gang.

Six

I'd often wondered what form my first acceptance would take. I'd imagined a letter full of phrases like *an exciting new talent* and *we warmly welcome you to the ranks of our contributors* and *do come and have lunch with me when next you visit London*; in the event what I got was a smudgy galley proof with a request on a compliment slip to correct and return by the 15th.

I still enjoy getting galley proofs but there won't, of course, be another one like the first. I shan't ever again have kippers for breakfast in the house in Orkney Terrace with *Lili* on the radio and poor old Gilbert Harding's latest outburst front page news. I shan't ever again live with anyone like my father who, when I showed him the galley proof, said, bewildered: 'But they've sent you the bloody thing back.' I don't recollect this with amused superiority. I don't see why he should have been conversant with the details of publication.

'How much will they pay you, then?' he asked me.

'Eight guineas, I think.'

'My God,' he said, 'that's a good week's wages.'

And in those days it was; from then onwards he started to brag about me. Not long after he made enquiries about central heating; that summer a solid fuel central heating system was installed and he partitioned the bedroom which Lester and I shared into two rooms. He might have done this whether or not my piece had been accepted; Amelia tended to be chesty, and of course it added to the value of the property. But it was to make all the difference to me in the two years of hard labour that lay ahead.

For Miranda had already worked out her plans for me. I took the proof to her at the Grange that evening and for the first time met her husband Max. He was a tall, heavily built man in his fifties, with faded blue eyes which looked straight past me. He mumbled 'How d'you do', held out his hand, mumbled something about having work to do, and went through a door on the other side of the hall.

Miranda smiled. 'There's a bottle of fine old authoritative port awaiting him in there,' she said. 'Come on, sweetie. Let's get down to it.'

There was something new in the room: two large black First Empire candlesticks with a sphinx at the base. I went over to them.

'Yes,' she said, 'I got them since you were last here. They're hideous, but quite genuine. And they suit the room.' She held out her hand and I gave her the galley. 'It's a big moment, isn't it?'

'I can't describe it. It's – it's – ' My voice trailed off.

'Ah, but some day you'll have to describe it. You'll have to describe everything. Max, now – he pays forty guineas for his suits, and they look like five-guinea reach-me-downs. He takes reasonable care of them, but clothes aren't important to him. So they take their revenge. It's things like that you've got to notice . . .' She waved towards the drinks. 'And pour me a Scotch, there's a dear.' She put the galley down on the coffee table. 'Just a couple of misprints here.' She gave me a pen – 'I think it was a golden Parker rollball – and indicated the misprints. 'Ring here, line in the margin, initial here – OK/TM.'

'I can't thank you enough,' I said. I sat down and sipped the whisky.

'Thank me by doing something with your talent. Don't do what I have done. For Christ's sake, keep on writing, no matter what you feel like. Don't keep a diary, don't write long letters – they're all substitutes for real work.' She stopped and lit two cigarettes and handed one over to me. Her silver and gold blouse was open to her considerable cleavage and her legs were unusually well-shaped, but I didn't, as I usually would have done, mentally unbutton the blouse to her waist and lift the skirt beyond her stocking-tops.

'It's a question of time,' I said.

'You've got to make time. Darling, I've got time, but what do I do? Buy First Empire candlesticks and read books I've read before and plan meals and now and again get mildly pissed and now and again – ' She stopped. 'I wonder why I can talk to you like this? You're so young, and you're a man. But I can talk to you about anything . . .'

'I can with you.' I put something of this into the relationship of my first hero with his mistress; but that was founded firmly upon sex. This wasn't: which was why it was so flattering.

'Good. Then we'll talk about what you're going to do with yourself. You're not academic, you know. I still have a few friends and you could get your Matric easily enough, and go on to the university. But you'll have to cram a lot of stuff you'll never need again. There isn't the time. And there's always the risk you'll end up teaching or on the BBC.'

'I wouldn't mind the BBC.'

'Death in life, my dear. I've seen it ruin more writers . . . You'd be better off at your father's shop, believe me. If only you were tough enough, that would be the very best thing. You'll mix with ordinary people all the time – and they're the ones you've got to write about. The thing is, they're hell to live with, you get so bloody lonely.'

'The artist has to be lonely.'

'Oh yes, darling, I believed that at your age. But loneliness leads to marriage. And children. And no time at all – because you've got to care too much about your job, you're stuck in one place. No, there's only one thing for it. Journalism.'

'I haven't even my School Cert. – '

'You can learn shorthand and typing – that's the one chore. Just one chore. You keep on being published in national papers and I'll get you a job. Somewhere in the Provinces at first. You want to leave home, don't you?'

'I thought London – '

'So did I once. The same London as you. *La Vie Bohème* and all that. But it doesn't exist, you know. Not until you've made it, not until you've become a Name.' She pronounced the last word with relish. 'All that stuff in *Moving Through* – pure wish-fulfilment. I suppose most first novels are. But it's no use me telling you, lovey. You want to go just the same.'

'That's what *The Chalk on the Elm*'s really about, isn't it?' I asked, referring to her third novel, which I had at long last got hold of.

'I didn't think anyone had read it,' she said. 'Yes, that's what it's about – how clever of you! But people don't want to read about disenchantment. You're in the enchantment business, my poppet, and don't you forget it. Most of the poor buggers' – I was becoming used to her language by now – 'who make up the reading public have quite enough disenchantment in their lives already. And booze is the hell of a price, and sex means messing about with Dutch caps or pacing the floor in the small hours with a wet squalling bundle. So there's us and the television and the flicks. It's all the same whether you like Tolstoy or Agatha Christie or *Hamlet* or *No Orchids for Miss Blandish*. The end-product's escape.'

'You mean you should try to give the public what it wants?'

'No, no,' she said impatiently. 'Give yourself what *you* want. You know about you – you don't know about anyone else. What do you want now? For Christ's sake get it!' She pointed in the direction of the hall. '*He*'s happy. He wanted an heir, he's got two sons. He wanted to make a lot of money: he's made a lot of money. And now all he wants is slowly to absorb the port his dear old dad put down for him. I sometimes wonder if I shouldn't buy him a television, it'd harm his liver less. Not that he'd have one in the house . . . Well, it's his liver . . .' She stabbed a red-painted finger-nail at me. 'But what about God, though? Is that what you want?'

'No, honestly.' I loosened my collar: it was very warm, and this time I was drinking more whisky than last time. 'That doesn't mean anything to me. I just want to look at things. And listen to people.'

'You'll think about it some day, though. God and all that. It's in your face. And that's the most destructive of all. I knew a man once – oh hell, he was my lover for six weeks – and he was a poet. Rudy Esher, you won't have heard of him. He became a monk. A bloody monk. I ask you! On his knees day and night – for what? What good does it do? He had plenty of money, he'd been all over

84

the world, and his poetry had something. *You're not safe here where voices are polite Though you may have escaped the night which staggers Scowling outside like a drunken bruiser, Its breath smelling of eternity* . . . But that was early stuff . . . He didn't use to talk about eternity with me . . .' She lit two more cigarettes and passed me one.

'If you write about something well enough, it's there, it's fixed, it won't go bad, though.' I was almost frightened to speak; she was so much more clever than I was, had had so much wider a life.

'Oh yes. Yes, dear Tommy. Look at *Ulysses* and look at almost everything else published that year, and you'll see the difference.'

The conversation turned to literature, with which I felt rather more at ease; I didn't want merely to sit in silence, but when she launched out into personal confidences I wasn't sure what my answer had to be. I wasn't used to people revealing themselves quite as frankly as Miranda, and I had a mounting fear of saying the wrong thing and being cut off from her suddenly. Above all, at eighteen, one has a great fear of making a fool of oneself, of being too absurdly shocked or of parading a sophistication which one doesn't really possess. But as we talked, I felt more and more at my ease.

Was it a mother-and-son relationship? Not precisely: for in that there would have been elements of guilt and shame. We weren't lovers and we were more than friends: we were teacher and pupil and I was her only pupil. I was very lucky: Max never interfered with our relationship. Perhaps he was perceptive enough to grasp the fact that we weren't and never would be lovers. But I think not: he simply wasn't interested in whether we were or not. What Dr Johnson called confusion of progeny would have been a different matter, feeling as he did about the family name. But a disastrous miscarriage had made Miranda incapable of conceiving again.

Her sterility had also turned him off sexually, though I wasn't aware of this at the time I met him. It wasn't merely that he thought of a wife as primarily a producer of heirs; he had the not uncommon belief that sex, unless indulged in only in the strictest moderation, was not only unbecoming to a man of his age but positively harmful. About every three months he'd knock gently at her bedroom door; but he stayed for so short a time that she never counted it as making love at all. He was merely exercising his marital rights, claiming what was his due. Perhaps too – as far as I can see inside his mind – he wanted to assure himself of his virility. I think it was essential to him to know that should the need arise he could produce heirs again.

That evening I had vague intimations of all this; already there was a part of me which never went off duty, never stopped making notes.

It was a cold night – spring came late in Engelsea – and the room was very warm. But all four bars of the electric fire were switched on; I began to sweat. And there is another difference between those days and now: our clothes were heavier and one had more of them, winter and summer.

'Take your jacket off, for Christ's sake,' Miranda said. 'Why sweat if you don't need to?'

I took it off; the action seemed oddly significant.

'And why not that woolly pullover?' she asked.

But I shook my head; my flannels weren't a very good fit and I was wearing braces.

She shrugged. 'Sweat if you want to, then.' She switched off three bars of the electric fire. 'I like my interiors warm.

You'll go to America one day, you know, and then you'll stop wearing woolly pullovers. I wonder what's to be done with you?'

'You said journalism.'

'Did I?'

'And to learn shorthand and typing.'

'I am bossy, aren't I?' I noticed how white and even her teeth were; I didn't know then that they were all capped at great expense.

'I don't mind.'

'No, you don't, my dear. You'll never mind anything which helps you get what you want. The question is whether your parents will mind.'

'My stepmother won't care either way. My father might be a bit puzzled.'

'Your stepmother?'

'My mother died when I was eight. Heart attack.'

'Oh yes, you told me . . . You're lucky. Working-class mums – in fact all mums – can be smothering. You've got enough on your plate without having to fight off your mum . . . Oh Christ, I hope I haven't shocked you.'

'Only a little.'

'I never mind what I say to anyone much. I'm always quite nice to Max, though, because he's my meal-ticket. Do you despise me for that?'

'It makes sense. Nothing's any better for being poor.'

'You sound very grown-up at times. Is your stepmother a wicked stepmother?'

I laughed. 'No. I quite like her.'

'You might have had some hellish neuroses if you didn't. And they can be useful to a writer. Of course they can cripple him too. Doesn't much matter if they bugger up his sex-life – we all have our crosses to bear – but they might well bugger up his writing.'

'They leave me alone,' I said. 'They're mainly interested in each other.'

'Still in business, are they?'

I hadn't heard the expression used in this way before but guessed what she meant. 'Very much so, I should think.'

'Really. I feel a bit envious. Fancy her yourself?'

'You don't know my father. He'd break my neck. Anyway, she must be forty if she's a day – ' I broke off. For the first time since I'd met her I was genuinely embarrassed.

She smiled. 'Don't worry. It's quite normal for you to feel that at your age. And of course there'll be a kind of incest barrier. It serves me right for being so bloody personal. But it doesn't seem to matter with you . . .'

I noticed properly for the first time the shape of her face. It was oval with a strong but not heavy jawline; that shape of face stays young longer because there isn't the tendency to sag that there is in a round face. For a moment we were silent; not because we had nothing to say but because it was enough to be in each other's company. It was a moment of danger; a move from either of us could have made the relationship physical and spoilt it. It was a moment of complete contentment, of a shared tranquillity. We were knowing and loving one another, we filled each other's thoughts. I have had a great deal from life, infinitely more than most people, and I've enjoyed it all. But there is nothing for which I am more grateful than that moment with Miranda all those years ago; for both of us, if only for a moment, wanted only to give to the other.

There wasn't any question she could have asked me which I wouldn't have answered truthfully; and from that moment onwards I don't believe that I ever told her a lie.

She was of course exactly what I needed at that period: I often wonder if I don't need someone like her now. More and more I feel that there's a gap in my life which can only be filled by someone of superior wisdom and greater strength, someone to whom my attitude will be not far short of worship. I've found no-one since Miranda: when it came down to it, all the candidates I chose for her position simply wanted something from me, if only to admire me and look up to me. I have never found this unpleasant, naturally: but I want someone to admire and look up to. I need a queen or a king, but preferably a queen. I need to give a special kind of love.

The moment when our relationship established itself passed, the silence was replaced by questions which carried on from where we had left off at my last visit. She asked me about my siblings; she made no comment when I answered her immediately by telling her what I felt about Lester and Amelia, but I knew that she was impressed; the word isn't as recondite as all that but no-one would have picked it up at eighteen who hadn't the collector's instinct for words.

'It's better than I thought,' she said finally. 'Almost made to measure for a writer. You have the experience of family life, which one really can't do without, but there's nothing to tie you down. Your father doesn't have a *thing* about the family business, does he?'

'Not him. He says it's better than working. I expect Lester will take over if I don't want it.'

'Not that it's entirely a bad thing to work in a shop. You see lots of people and you can dream your own dreams. Better than journalism in a way. But you can't stay in Engelsea.'

'You're content here, though.'

'Content?' She frowned. There were lines on her forehead I'd not noticed before. 'I've declared a separate peace, my darling Tommy.'

It was the first time I'd heard anyone use the phrase, though I recognized its source.

'And I'm going into battle?'

She looked at her watch. 'Yes, my love. And it's a dirty, desperate battle.' She stood up. 'I'm tired.' She kissed me briefly on the cheek. 'I'll see you at the Coble on Saturday.'

The audience was over. As I went out I realized that I felt tired too. I was happy but I was tired. I turned my overcoat collar up against the wind. I remember that overcoat well; it was at least twice the weight of overcoats today, in a thick brown Melton, belted, with a deep collar, and extending well below the knee. There was something military about it; certainly at a pinch it would have served as a blanket.

A dirty, desperate battle; the metaphor was in my mind as I strode out along the Filey Road, the taste of whisky in my mouth. That long straight road bordered by the sea was not one of my favourite walks: indeed, because of its absence of any features of the least interest, it always rather depressed me. But that evening I had everything before me; I didn't believe that the battle would be dirty and desperate, but triumphant and splendid. I was too young to realize how it had crippled Miranda.

Seven

The cheque arrived by the same post as the copy of *Vanguard* containing my article. To this day it gives me pleasure to receive cheques and to see myself in print; on that morning in Engelsea it's no more than the simple truth to say that there was no happiness in my life which had ever come near it. It was all the greater because it was my first success of any kind.

I think that only Amelia had any notion of what having the article published meant to me. Her face went pink with excitement and she turned and kissed me. 'Tom! Clever Tom! Tom's written a *story*! In real print!' she said; which, when I come to think of it, exactly summarizes my own feelings. But the others looked at it briefly, with that curious expression I've often noticed on the face of non-readers, as if encountering some unfamiliar species of animal which they suspected might be dangerous.

I suppose this reaction was partly due to the rather forbidding appearance of *Vanguard*, the typography of which hadn't changed very much since it was founded by a group of minor Fabians in 1910. It was half literary and half political; it had always been its policy to keep politics out of the literary half, which was probably the main reason for its survival. It was a good place to begin from, though the *New Statesman* might have been a shade better. The leader article was thick with words like *rapprochement* and *détente* and *bi-partisan* and the list of contents included articles on Mauriac and Cocteau and Picasso; to my father and Hetty along with ninety per cent of the population it might as well have been written in Sanskrit.

The cheque was a different matter. 'My God!' my father said, 'all for a bit of scribbling. Well, lad, it's better than working.'

'You should put it away for your holidays,' Hetty said.

'Put it away be damned!' my father said. 'Spend it before they've found out they've made a mistake.'

'They haven't made a mistake,' I said. 'And that's nothing to what you can get from American magazines.'

'I always said you had a headpiece on you if only you'd learn to use it,' my father said. 'You get it from your mother, she always had her nose stuck in a book.'

I noticed Hetty frown: she didn't like my mother to be mentioned. But my father – I realize now both how annoying and how endearing this insensitivity was to women – never noticed. He looked at the article again. 'There's no Clipper Street in Engelsea,' he said.

'I know. It's not specially supposed to be Engelsea. It's any little seaside town.'

'You're no fool. Nobody can get at you then, can they?'

'That's the idea.'

'Will you buy me a present, clever Tom?' Amelia asked, sitting on my knee. 'You're the cleverest boy in the whole world.'

Hetty smiled. 'Cheeky! She knows how to get round the men already.'

'I'll buy you a lovely present,' I said. For I did at that moment feel that I was the cleverest boy in the whole world. That was just what I wanted to hear.

I bought the present for Amelia, a small pink teddy bear I knew that she'd been hankering after, at my cousin Jesse Rimswell's shop. Jesse was a rather plump young man in his early thirties whose cropped hair and gold-rimmed glasses gave him an oddly sinister appearance. His shop was at that time the only newsagents in Engelsea and in addition sold sweets and tobacco and toys and stationery and bric-à-brac of all kinds; it was in a good position midway between the fishermen's quarter and the newer part of the town, and only my grandparents had more money than Jesse. And that was because they'd been in business longer and had picked up more land at lower prices.

Jesse was a lay preacher and didn't smoke or drink; he was strenuously cheerful as was his wife Madge, who occasionally served in the shop when she wasn't occupied with their six children. My father didn't like him very much; he said that like all these bloody Nonconformists he was hypocritical and randy and gluttonous and would take the pennies off a dead man's eyes; but already he was of great fascination to me precisely because he was so different from myself. Even then I didn't feel myself able to afford the luxury of moral judgements; and though now there are quite a few people whom I'd like to see hanged it isn't a question of morals but of survival – it's them or me.

Jesse was a source of fascination to me in another way. There were more different kinds of things in his shop than in any other in Engelsea. His shop seemed fuller of articles at every visit. I'm sure that he sold all of them eventually; he had the born shopkeeper's instinct for what people wanted, and though the shop was crammed with objects it was never untidy or scruffy and had always a faint pleasant smell of newsprint and chocolate.

The sun had come out that morning, but there was a cold wind. The sign outside the shop was creaking; it was a curiously melancholy sound. Jesse was reading what I recognized as a copy of *Vanguard*. For the first time I saw the magazines and newspapers on the counter and in the racks behind the door as the manifestations of a different world, a larger world than Engelsea. And I had entered it. But to stay in it, one day to live in it. depended upon how clearly I could see Engelsea, how clearly I could see Jesse, how clearly I could see the shop and everything in it.

And without Miranda's advice I might have continued for years to write unpublishable short stories and finally an unpublishable novel. I might well have still been in Engelsea, drinking a lot and dreaming a lot, reading a lot in between, but only for escape. There's someone like that in every small town, talented because he has a large stock of knowledge which may occasionally be useful or diverting, but never to be taken seriously. They're generally nicknamed Professor. Their only hope of escape is somehow or other to acquire a professional qualification, to become at least a teacher or a librarian, but drinking and dreaming and the long dusty grind of examinations are difficult to reconcile. And even then the bitterness would remain.

They say genius will out. I've never believed it myself. If a potential heavyweight champion loses an arm he's not going to be a boxer, and that's that. And if a writer goes in the wrong direction at an early age, he's not going to be a writer. If I hadn't sent that story to Miranda that morning, I wouldn't have been in Jesse's shop buying a teddy bear for Amelia and a pound box of liquorice all-sorts for Lester and a pound box of Black Magic for Hetty and twenty Manikin cheroots for my father; and Jesse, looking up from *Vanguard*, wouldn't have said in perfect seriousness: 'One of these days people'll boast of having known you, Tom.'

I've never forgotten that: it had the unexpected effect of bringing tears to my eyes.

'Nice of you to say so,' I mumbled.

He looked at the teddy bear. 'You spoil that child,' he said. 'Wait.' He rummaged beneath the counter. 'I'll do it up properly.' He wrapped it up in pink flowered gift paper and tied it up with red ribbon. 'She'll like that. Pretty wrapping's half the fun for a little girl.' He hesitated, then rapidly wrapped up the others in gold wrapping paper. 'We won't spoil the ship for a ha'porth of tar.'

He gave me my change. I looked at it. 'How much –'

'My treat,' he said. 'Mind, you want to look after your money. You haven't won the football pools, you know.' But as he spoke he was caressing Amelia's gift; I had the sensation of being inside his shoes. I realized what it was to have his vocation. I didn't want to evaluate that vocation: it was enough to understand it.

I expected that evening at the Coble to be a festival, I expected some sort of accolade, full fellowship of Miranda's Gang, in fact to be granted commissioned rank. (For in every social group, no matter how informal, there are grades.)

Before I went in I stood by the seawall, the copy of *Vanguard* in my hand, for a full half-hour; I wanted to delay the pleasure, to savour it in advance, to prepare appropriate responses to the congratulations which were about to be heaped upon me. It had turned cold but I didn't feel it; I felt slightly sick with excitement, but physical considerations were unimportant. I saw a lifetime of triumph ahead of me; I had begun to be a name.

But when I entered the Lounge Bar and saw with that curious twinge which is generally described as being in the pit of the stomach but is in fact, though non-sexual, in the genitals, that Miranda's Gang was already there, no-one greeted me except Ralph Thoralby, who raised his pint-pot and mumbled in my direction.

Miranda didn't look at me; she was reading a letter which Harvey Abington had just given to her.

I sat down opposite her, the copy of *Vanguard* in my hand.

'It's out today,' I said.

'Of course he doesn't understand,' she said to Harvey, seeming not to hear me. 'It's the typical Eng. Lit. approach. He's always seen writers in terms of movements with a capital M, and he can't realize what a load of bloody nonsense it all is. But don't you say that. Be very humble. Say you appreciate the soundness of his approach, but that you think the time is ripe to consider new methods. But for Christ's sake say you're sorry that you jumped the gun, and that you'd value his opinion. Buy the old sod a meal or a drink.'

She turned to me. 'What's out today?'

'*Vanguard.*'

'Of course.' She smiled. 'It's a big moment, isn't it?' She tapped the article with her finger. 'How many times have you read it now?'

'About a hundred.'

Harvey looked at the article. It didn't seem to take him very long; but I could almost hear the click as each line was photographed in his brain.

'Not bad,' he said. 'Decadent, of course. But then it's a

96

thoroughly decadent periodical. Pays lip service to the idea of class warfare, has a good old weep about the suffering proletariat now and again, but actually makes its profits from the exploitation of individual sensitivity.'

'What else is literature about?' I asked.

'It doesn't matter what it's *about*. It's what it's for. Its purpose, my dear chap, is to advance the class struggle.'

'Fuck the class struggle,' Miranda said. 'Why can't you say something nice about the boy's article?'

'It's competent enough,' Harvey said. 'Bloody good for a kid his age. But he's already decadent. It's absolutely obvious that he doesn't give a toss about the workers.'

'Neither do I,' Miranda said.

'My sweet,' he said, his voice changing tone, 'that's just not true. I know what your record is, and I know how much you help now.' The harshness had gone from his voice and the accent was even more emphatically that of an officer and a gentleman.

'She's helped *me*,' I said.

'She'll help you to be a prosperous bourgeois hack who one day will forget the people he came from.'

Now there was anger in his voice; I realized that this conversation was important to him. He had to make an impression with the Gang, just as he had to make an impression as a WEA lecturer. Since then he's become a Labour MP and television personality and, in the process, reasonably well-off. We run across each other from time to time – London's a small place – but I never refer to his Communist phase.

I listened to him that night, though, and took mental notes. Whenever I've depicted a Communist in a novel, they've always been based on Harvey at this stage in his career. I didn't bother to argue with him – he was even then by way of being a professional talker, and I would have been hopelessly outclassed. I realized, above all, that what he said about me was in an important respect true. I didn't give a toss about the workers, I didn't give a toss about politics. I think now that if I'd not met Miranda and through her the Gang, I might well have been led through reading and loneliness and the spirit of the times to believe that politics had something to give me, that a change in the system of government might significantly change my life.

But Harvey cured me of that. And Jane Badingham, who'd been sitting in silence over an Advocaat, suddenly broke into the conversation and said something which I've never forgotten.

'Do what you want to, darling,' she said. 'You're the only person who knows. Even if it kills you, do what you want to.'

'That's dangerous advice,' Ralph Thoralby said. 'At this moment I want to put my hand down your blouse.'

She shrugged. Her white blouse, through which pink underwear was visible, was extremely low-cut; the shrug forced up her breasts. 'If you really want to, you will. Go on, I won't stop you.'

I watched their faces. Miranda was frowning slightly. Jane was looking at Miranda. Harvey's face had a rather shy, amused expression. Ralph's face was non-committal. The others in the group, aware that something was happening, were turning to watch Jane. Ralph stretched out his hand across the table. There was silence. Then he waved his hand away. 'You're a cock-teaser, darling Jane,' he said. 'Take the will for the deed.'

'She'll do that once too often,' Miranda said. Jane stared at her, faintly smiling, somehow triumphant; I was seized by wonder at the marvellous complexity of human relationships; hard on its heels came a fear that there wouldn't even be time enough to understand it. I'd already forgotten that I'd expected to be praised, to be made much of, that evening; now I didn't care what impression I made, I wanted merely to watch and to listen.

There weren't any formal introductions to the Gang except on the few occasions when Miranda brought Names to Engelsea. But before the evening was out I managed to introduce myself to everyone there whom I didn't know already. Bill Abercorn and his first wife Nina, Roy Badgeworth and his fiancée Kim Cressage, Jack Barrington, Cyril Abbott, Jean Pritchett – their faces and voices and the way they dressed all comes back to me now. Bill, tall and bulky, with a baby face and huge forehead, was an actor who was resting and trying to write a play. He was living on Nina's earnings as a secretary; Nina was small and slim and timid and Bill was apt to bully her. Roy was a primary school teacher who'd done several talks on the BBC; he was a precise, neat little man (smaller than me) with rimless spectacles. Kim was the same size – as if made to order for him – with nondescript features but wonderful legs. Jack Barrington was an accountant with a Scottish accent and literary ambitions which so far he'd mainly gratified by articles for the *Dalesman* and *Yorkshire Observer Budget*. He was, however, writing a novel. Cyril Abbott was chief reporter for the *Engelsea Clarion*, and his girl-friend Jean Pritchett was a librarian at County HQ. They were keen on the theatre; the chief manifestation of this keenness was their piercingly loud voices, meticulously going up at the end of each sentence. They were both tall and fair-haired and almost excessively healthy-looking; I might have fancied Jean but for her height.

Out of the whole Gang present that evening only Bill and Harvey and I have amounted to anything, become

Names. And when I describe them, they don't seem a very impressive lot. But with the exception of Ralph Thoralby they were all young, they were all reasonably well-read and well-informed, they all had their *ambitions,* secret or avowed. They were all middle-class or on the way to being middle-class; and with the exception of Ralph Thoralby, they were all Left-Wing. Whatever political opinions Ralph had, he kept to himself. Sooner or later I discovered the secret ambitions of other members of the Gang: I never discovered Ralph's. I don't think he had any; I believe now that he was content to go through life with the minimum of effort extracting whatever pleasure he could on the way. He enjoyed his job as English teacher at the nearby grammar school, but I don't think that he was by any means dedicated to it.

But this is to look at the Gang too coldly. For never before or since has any group of people given me so much happiness. There is no-one so lonely as the young man with literary ambitions in a small town like Engelsea, particularly if he's been educated at a secondary modern school. I made no friends at school; I wasn't persecuted, but I simply couldn't mix. I wasn't any good at games, either; I've often regretted this as being now an unfillable gap in my experience. Maurice was my only real friend and occasionally with him I would be included in invitations to parties, generally given by a Knossington or relative of a Knossington. But the Knossingtons' social life was centred round the Chapel, and the Chapel wasn't for me.

It all boiled down to the question of what one talked about; and at this stage in my life I only wanted to talk about literature and writing. Later I learned the language of ordinary people and less and less mixed with literary people. *Ordinary people* sounds patronizing and isn't accurate; but the *real people,* the expression I use privately, can only be used in public by a politician with a very strong stomach. It doesn't really matter; what is important is that until now I've always chosen for my material people in whose lives literature – or any of the arts – plays no important part.

This was something which Miranda taught me. 'You may not like ordinary people,' she said to me once. 'I doubt whether they like you. But they're the ones you've got to write about. If you want to sink without trace, make the hero of your first novel a sensitive young writer in a small Yorkshire town. Because where the hell do you go on from there?'

She was quite right, of course; but that doesn't affect what I felt about the Gang; and still do after nearly twenty years. With them I was free to speak my mind as I was with no-one else. They were determinedly broad-minded and progressive; no subject was barred. I suppose that those evenings at the Coble were my substitute for the university, with Miranda as the faculty. I don't think that I had a bad education; and I avoided the examination treadmill.

The Gang helped to make me; I think now that it helped to break Miranda. It prevented her from entering fully into the social life of Engelsea and taking new material from there; she did her duty as Max's wife, but no more. The longer a writer is silent, the harder it is to start again; land is all the better for lying fallow, but not talent. Without the Gang, loneliness and boredom, if nothing else, might have forced her back to her desk. But the adoration the Gang gave her so unstintingly, the pleasure of arranging the lives of its members for them, of being their queen and their oracle, came to replace the grind of creation.

And the reviews of her last novel had hurt her more

than she cared to admit. What was more, the tone of reviewing had become perceptibly nastier since then. Adverse reviews once were at the worst mildly disappointed, trying even then to find something to praise; now they were full of a savage hatred, as if the subject of the review had not only written an inferior book but had been guilty of some loathsome crime. And for some reason the hatred would be all the more savage if the author concerned had, like Miranda, ever written a bestseller.

Perhaps too she didn't dare to risk failure because of what it would have done to her standing in the eyes of the Gang. Perhaps she could all too clearly visualize them in the Lounge Parlour of the Coble whispering over the reviews, loyally deploring the reviewers' malignant stupidity when she came in or, worse still, keeping silent. They wouldn't be her subjects any longer, they wouldn't be her courtiers, they'd be a kind of a tribunal.

I can see all this now; I couldn't then. I simply took all that she and the Gang had to give me. And as soon as I was away from her, kicked away the ladder I'd climbed on, I made my duty visits – which were no more than an excuse for me to boast about my triumphs – and went back to my own life. I've never been troubled by a sense of guilt, though I understand it well enough for professional purposes. Mostly, to use another writer's phrase, I see myself as a camera, and who ever heard of a guilty camera?

I've avoided guilt until now, just as I've avoided writing directly about my own experience. I haven't looked at myself. There are enough people in that line of business, parading their own sensitivity, watching with fascination what they term their spiritual development. They believe in – if I've got the correct phrase – agonized self-appraisal, searching of the psyche at the deepest level, the imposition of a pattern upon their experience.

I don't believe that the writer has any business to look at himself at all. I only want now to remember Miranda; but as I remember her I'm forced to ask myself if I loved her enough. I took, and it was right that I should take. But when the time came that I was in a position to give, did I give enough?

Eight

And yet as I look back I look back only with joy. This was the time when I first started to look at people and places and things systematically. I'd been looking – looking with delight and astonishment – all my life, but in fits and starts, my vision blurred by half-digested theories.

'Nothing else counts, darling,' Miranda said to me, 'except making the reader see and feel and smell and hear. Don't ever let me catch you thinking. Any fool with a degree can think. Harvey talks about writing a novel, you know. He'll get it published, but it won't be any good. He's too clever; he has too many theories. And he's too cold. You're a cold little bastard in many ways, but not about the things which matter. And I don't mean social injustice and all that crap either.'

I understand all this perfectly now, but at the time I couldn't take it all in, I obeyed my instincts rather than my intelligence. But imperceptibly a worry was removed. I didn't think that I was going mad, but more and more, comparing myself with the people around me, I'd begun to feel that there was something wrong, that my impressions of the world about me were too vivid, too keenly sensed, too unselective, but I'd reached the stage where a length of wood in the basement of my father's shop was as important to me as a sunset or a rainbow or a swooping seagull. I couldn't see any physical object, animate or inanimate, as being drab; I was hooked on reality.

At the age I was then, sex complicated it. At eighteen one is almost permanently sexually excited. And in my case almost permanently sexually repressed. I was occasionally invited to parties; I took two girls out to the cinema and one to a dance, but got no further than a good-night kiss.

The fact is that I wasn't a member of any group except Miranda's Gang, and there weren't any available girls in Miranda's Gang. Very few people meet the opposite sex except as members of a group and – unwisely I now consider – I elected not to join the Nonconformist group. A little boredom wouldn't have hurt me, I should have acquired a great deal of material which now I can never acquire, and I should have known more girls. And I might even amongst the boredom have caught a glimpse of what gave some of the older ones in particular a genuine serenity.

Miranda wouldn't have approved of me joining the Nonconformists, of course. When she thought about it, which wasn't very often, she was an atheist. She wasn't militant about it, but she would have thought of attendance at the Methodist chapel as being a betrayal of my vocation. And Nonconformism wasn't intellectually respectable either. A conversion to Catholicism she might have accepted at a pinch; it was, in her own words, so 'gloriously barbaric, so splendidly reactionary, so fascist and incense-reeking'. (This was over twenty years ago.)

My loneliness, the feeling of being cut off apart from Miranda's Gang, she positively approved of. 'Darling, you'll have to get used to being on your tod. You'll be on your tod your whole life, and never more than when you're married. It has its compensations.'

In the meantime I was in a state of sexual repression. I don't think that it did me any great harm – it's even possible that it gave a sharper edge to my writing. There were means, voluntary or involuntary, of relief, but they're too dreary to be worth recalling. What I remember is how attractively packaged girls were then. Perhaps it's the distance of time that does it, but they wore brighter colours, their hair shone more, their skins were cleaner, and they wore suspenders and fully-fashioned stockings, so that even the primmest was a whore beneath her skirts. Even though skirts covered the knees there were always revelations, accidental or intentional; with luck, for instance, a journey on a double-decker bus could provide a glimpse of white flesh, the memory of which would carry one happily through the day.

There was a mystique about women's underwear then which doesn't seem to exist now to the same degree. I remember the way in which I'd surreptitiously peep at the window of Sue Knossington, Draper. What was almost intolerably exciting was that the garments there would cover girls' bare flesh; that knickers, above all, would cover that portion of the female anatomy which was never very long out of my mind. The fact that it's hairy, sometimes exuberantly so, was a bonus, real gold on the lily.

I did know all the facts of life; what I'd picked up at school was augmented by reading and the evenings with Miranda's Gang, who made a point, if not a fetish, of being frank. All except Ralph assumed that everyone knew the mechanics of the most complicated perversions; but Ralph would always take the trouble to explain. Perhaps it was the consequence of his being a teacher, perhaps it was the desire to corrupt. Miranda was more likely to direct one to a book if she saw any indication of ignorance on my face – which then revealed my thoughts far more transparently than it does now.

I expect that this was one of my main attractions as far as Miranda was concerned. I was someone whom she could mould, whom she could make into her own creation. No doubt she loved her sons, but from the little she said about them they took after Max in having no literary inclinations whatever. I bought a typewriter – an Oliver portable, I remember – and soon picked up a fair speed. Shorthand was more difficult; it wasn't simply a matter of learning the outlines but of getting practice.

Maurice would help me here from time to time, but I was seeing far less of him. He was occupied with his studies and had a girl friend now, Maureen Ballater, a tall plump bouncing girl with a great deal of soft brown hair and what is described as an outgoing personality. He'd met her at the College – which was more and more becoming the centre of his life – and to add to his problems she was a Catholic. I hadn't thought of him having problems before; but there was money trouble at home, his father's coal business having struck a rough patch, and he was beginning to be subject to blinding headaches. On top of this there were periods when he couldn't keep his food down; amongst it all he had to keep abreast of a crowded syllabus, with examinations always looming over him. Maurice had a retentive memory and a well-ordered mind; but he was a slow thinker and incapable of taking short cuts or of bluffing his way through when he didn't know his subject.

Maureen was much quicker and livelier, with a rather sardonic sense of humour. I was inclined to envy him his possession of her; I knew instinctively that they didn't sleep together, but it was evident also that they derived great comfort from each other, that theirs was a mature relationship.

As I grow older, I value my friendship with Maurice more and more. He's the only person I know whom I'm positive would always behave decently in all circumstances, and the only person I know in whom there is no trace of envy. If we'd seen more of each other during this period of my life, my morals might have been a little less shoddy, I might have been saved many mistakes, I might have been the giver – and recipient – of more love.

The hero's friend in my first novel isn't Maurice, except in patches. Apart from any other consideration, I couldn't then manage to portray simple goodness. I've always had enough sense not to try to bite off more than I can chew; in literature no A's for Effort are awarded.

At the time I wrote my first novel I had just begun to understand something about Maurice. But at eighteen I was chiefly concerned with surfaces. For company there was Miranda's Gang; and I wrote my pieces of what I called reportage, I tussled one evening a week with shorthand, I went to the cinema, almost always by myself, and I wandered round Engelsea consciously observing. Occasionally I went further afield to Filey and Bridlington and Scarborough and as far as York; and now and again I was taken by my father to visit my grandparents in Charbury. That was before the older part of Charbury was, to use the planners' euphemism, redeveloped; in that maze of narrow cobbled streets dominated by mill chimneys, I knew, though only half-consciously, that I'd found the kind of background which suited me best. But not until he took my grandparents to Ilkley one day in June did I decide, or it was decided for me, where I'd set my first novel.

Which is not to say that the town in my book is Ilkley.

Real places – or any one place – are too limiting for fiction. I put features from other small towns into the town in my novel. This in one sense has nothing to do with Miranda. In another sense it has everything to do with her. For I couldn't have looked properly at Ilkley or anywhere else if she hadn't taught me to observe, if she hadn't encouraged me to write only about what I observed.

A picture stays with me. We are sitting on a rug near the Cow and Calf. The sun is hot but there's a cool breeze. My father is lying on his back, his eyes half-closed; even in that position full of fierce energy. My grandparents are sitting bolt upright, watching Amelia buttoning a dress on Snow Baby. My grandfather wears a blue trilby hat and a navy blue suit and an open-necked white shirt, the collar outside the jacket. My grandmother has a pink flowered hat and dark green print dress. There's a smell of camphor and cachous and pipe smoke and trodden grass. Hetty, in a green dress and fully-fashioned stockings, is getting something out of the van.

'She fair dotes on that funny old dolly,' my grandmother says.

My grandfather smiles. 'Shall us get thee a new dolly then, doy?' he says to Amelia.

Doy means darling; it's generally used only with children. I note this, and also the fact that though you can say a child's a little love or a little darling, you can't say he's a little doy. For some reason it's only used in the vocative case.

Lester is standing on top of the Calf, the large rock – I suppose an Ice Age boulder – with footholds in its side which stand beside the larger outcropping of the Cow. He turns to climb down, then bursts into tears. 'Mam!' he shouts. 'Mam! Help me!' But even as Hetty goes towards him my father is on his feet and halfway towards the rock. I follow him. My grandparents stay where they are. I know that I will use all this one day; the way that the road swoops down to level off at the cattle-grid at the bottom is particularly important.

In September I enrolled at nightschool for classes in shorthand and typing. Classes were held at my old school in Leonard Street, a large Victorian building overlooking the Front. It was strange to be going back there; it wasn't a place to which I felt the least sentimental attachment. It was in the sham Gothic style with high arched windows in groups of lancets. It was a wet evening and the main hall where we enrolled smelled of chalk dust and ink and rubberized cloth. Nothing had changed: the Honours Board, the pine-wainscoted walls, the prints of Costumes of the World, retained their power to depress me. One of my recurring nightmares was that I was back at school again; and here I was, nearly nineteen, a shop assistant, preparing to qualify myself for a job I felt certain at that moment I'd never get. My publications didn't seem to count any more. I was tired of the unremitting obligation to observe the world around me, I felt sure of nothing except that I was a failure.

I'm not given to depression: my vocation is to celebrate. Hit me and I'll hit you back, knock me down a hundred times and I'll get up a hundred and one times. I have always been glad to awake each morning because each morning I'm certain that today will be better than yesterday. For all that, there are moments when I feel that I've been ordered to make a long march over rough country in bad weather with a hard fight at the end of it. I suffered from this feeling more when I was young, because I didn't then have the certainty that I would recover from it, would settle down into the rhythm of the march, even welcoming the sting of the snow-laden wind on my face.

But that evening I wasn't even grateful for the presence of about a dozen young girls in brightly-coloured mackintoshes and headscarves. Three of them were fat, two of them thin, two of them excessively spotty; but one, a pale, dark-haired girl, was actually beautiful, and four of them I wouldn't, as the saying goes, have thrown out of my bed. They were girls and they were miraculous and I could smell their wonderful smell above the smell of wet clothes and chalk dust and ink, and under their clothes were the twelve dark mysteries, so comic and so poetic, so homely and so terrible, so simple and so complex, so ugly and so beautiful. And this added to my depression; I felt that somehow they knew what I felt, that not one of them would ever make herself accessible to me, that even the plain ones had come to the school that evening deliberately to taunt me.

The next morning there was a proof from the *New Statesman* in the post. Miranda had suggested – or rather had commanded – that I should publish somewhere else than *Vanguard*. 'Stick with the one paper, darling, and they take you for granted. And there's always a danger of you getting too used to their house style, so you can't write any other way. And then where are you if ever they get tired of you?'

I hadn't in fact written any differently for the *Statesman*, except that on Miranda's advice I'd put in references to Kafka and Rilke, which she said always disposed them favourably towards a writer. I didn't think that it made any difference, but Miranda thought that it did; that was the first time that I suspected her perceptions could be as flawed as anyone else's.

It didn't diminish my gratitude towards her and nothing could diminish my triumph. But somewhere in the back of my mind I briefly foresaw a moment when I should kick overboard the pilot and I had a vision of Miranda not as queen but as an ageing woman, her career over, her pupil growing away from her.

Lester, of all people, dispelled the slight sadness which this thought induced. Swallowing convulsively – he wasn't a dainty eater   he stared at me, then said in his hoarse voice: 'Mr Jackson read your essay in that book.' He pointed to a copy of *Vanguard* on the sideboard.

'Mr Jackson?'

'The English teacher, nit. He says you're very clever. Should be going to a university.'

'Tell him thank you.'

Lester piled butter and marmalade on his toast. 'I don't think you're clever. I think you're daft.'

'Hold your din,' his mother said. 'Tom is clever. I hope you're as clever.'

Amelia stuck her tongue out at Lester. I smiled at her and squeezed her hand.

'You won't go away, will you, Tom?' she asked me.

'I doubt it.' It wasn't true, but already her eyes were brimming with tears; I didn't want to upset her for the day.

My father said nothing until we were walking along the Front to the shop.

'I don't mind if you go to the university,' he said. 'Some of the buggers who do go are no brighter than you.'

'I don't want to. I want to be a journalist.' I paused, feeling rather shamefaced. 'A writer.'

'It's not easy. Your mate Mrs Abberwick doesn't write books any more, does she?'

'No,' I said, rather astounded at his knowing this.

'She has her husband to keep her. You'll be bloody lucky if you find a woman to keep you.'

'You never know your luck,' I said lightly. Another

theme of my first novel was emerging, though I didn't recognize it then.

'I do, lad. You'll addle your bread all your life, choose how. If you get a qualification now, you can write in your spare time. I don't think you're cut out for the shop.'

'I don't mind,' I said.

'You will one day.' He ruffled his short stubby hair, iron-grey now. 'Christ, I should have thought of this before.'

'I didn't know what I wanted to do before.'

'Before you met Mrs Abberwick.' He looked across the flower beds at the sun-sparkling sea. 'I suppose she put you against the university.'

'It wouldn't be right for me.'

'Are you sure you're not doing something for her?'

'She's forty, Dad.' I think I was genuinely shocked.

He laughed. 'I'd told you, women of forty keep it in the same place,' he said. 'Wouldn't do you any harm. Learn a lot from an older woman.'

Another theme for the first novel had emerged. On the surface level, though shocked, I was sexually excited by the idea. It wasn't something I'd ever thought of before. But creatively, deep down, I was excited in a different way.

'I have learned a lot,' I said. 'About writing. And about books.'

'Very nice too. But I'm your father. And I'm telling you something. Don't make a little tin god out of Mrs Abberwick. She may not always be right. Think about it, son.'

'All right,' I said: and off and on I did think about it all day until I was with Miranda's Gang in the Coble that night showing off the proof in a casual but conspicuous way, listening intoxicated to her words of praise, which were less restrained than usual.

'You're a pro, darling,' she said. 'A real old pro. Fucking marvellous, the way you've worked in good old Rilke and Kafka. You see what I mean about house style?'

'You're never wrong,' I said; and at that moment I really believed it.

Nine

I was the only man in both the typing and the shorthand classes – at first to my consternation, feeling my manhood somehow diminished. The tradition in Engelsea was that certain occupations, shorthand and typing among them, were exclusively for women, and I was curiously shy of explaining that I wanted to be a journalist.

I sat by myself at the back of the classroom, feeling that the dozen girls there were all giggling at me; none of them was above twenty, and at that age they take a great pleasure in embarrassing the opposite sex, particularly one so young as I was and still given to blushing. But after the first lesson they grew used to me and by then the word had passed round, Engelsea being a small place, that I was a published writer and I was looked upon with some awe or at least with a puzzled respect.

They grew used to me; I never quite grew used to the proximity of so many girls. Even the plain ones had the smell of women, the voices of women, and there were times when, looking away from the blackboard for a second, I could be entranced by the curve of a cheek, the whiteness of a neck, the smallness of a hand brushing hair back from the eyes. Seeing them at close quarters confirmed how stupid it was to categorize women as bedworthy or unbedworthy. Miranda had in any case made me see how adolescent this was.

'If you don't look at women clearly, dear heart,' she said, 'you'll never be a writer. You really mustn't look at some woman with her hair scraped up in a bun and wearing glasses and her skirts nearly down to her ankles, and say she'd be all right with a sack over her head. Just imagine her starkers with her hair down and her glasses off. The woman *you* see isn't the real woman.'

I didn't always take this advice, but before the third lesson I'd mentally undressed the plain ones too and found, paradoxically, that this was making me see them not only as objects of desire, but as individual beings; I noted scraps of their conversation and began to build up a store of information about women. Not that I looked at them asexually; my glands were still hard at work and from the second lesson onwards I always wore a double-breasted suit to hide the erections that would sometimes seize me even when my attention was entirely caught up by the intricacies of a grammalogue or by the jump of the quick brown fox.

The teacher, Mr Johnson, a rather wizened man in his mid-fifties who always wore a stiff white collar and a blue striped suit and the same blue spotted tie, I regarded as part of the classroom furniture. I learned from the girls later that he taught at a College of Commerce near Scarborough and was married with five children. He spoke with only a faint Yorkshire accent in a dry, monotonous voice; and if he had the same sexual fantasies about the girls as I had they certainly didn't register on his face. In fact no feelings of any sort registered themselves on his face; I forgot about him for years, then used the expression – or rather lack of it – in his face and voice for a minor character in my first novel.

But Cora Ramelton, the dark-haired girl I'd noticed on enrolment night, was the one who occupied most of my attention. I used her in my first novel too – she was the model for the rich man's daughter whom the hero makes pregnant. But the rich man's daughter wasn't Cora. To begin with, Cora wasn't a rich man's daughter, but a fisherman's daughter. Her hair wasn't black when I looked at it closely, but a very dark brown. Her eyes weren't hazel but grey-blue. She didn't have dimples; when not animated, her expression was inclined to be remote. She had a pale complexion, almost sallow; the skin of my character glowed with good health. She was very slim, almost skinny; my character would have been plump if she hadn't taken trouble with her diet. Most important of all, Cora was ambitious. She worked at Knossington's the drapers, but didn't intend to be a shopgirl all her working life. Nor did she intend to marry a fisherman. And my character, of course, wasn't in the least ambitious; she didn't have to be.

For the first three lessons I was quite content to glance at her from time to time and dream about her. I wanted her to be unattainable, *la princesse lointaine*. There were pictures in my mind of her and me on the headland on a stormy night, parting for ever, her dark hair streaming out behind her, her pale face, the tears glistening in her eyes, lit up from time to time as the beam from the lighthouse came round. I never quite worked out why we parted, except that violent death and great events and horsemen with high boots and scarlet cloaks were somehow involved.

Strangely enough, she was never the cause of any of my erections, nor the centre of any of my sexual fantasies. For *that*, almost any girl would serve my purpose.

My romantic tableaux were all silent. Cora's voice was not unpleasant, but her ambition drove her to attempt to speak Standard English. This meant that all her a's were broad and her other vowels narrow; the broad a's sounded merely affected, but the other vowels were positively grotesque. I had, and still have, a Yorkshire accent myself, but from listening to Miranda in particular I knew that though *butter*, for instance, has a narrow u, it isn't pronounced *better*, and that *bush* and *butcher* have a full u, indeed a Yorkshire u.

To make it worse, her enunciation was forced in the extreme, almost strangled; I hated listening to her because of the sense of strain it gave me. Some people would have been amused by it; but even at eighteen I found it pathetic. I didn't want to feel sorry for her and she made me feel sorry for her. And, I reflect now, it was in a way rather splendid; grotesque though she sounded, she was in there trying, she was doing what she could to change her life, as indeed I then was.

I might have remained content to dream about her, but on the fourth week of the course I arrived late and as I entered the classroom had a glimpse of the flesh above her stocking top (she'd just shifted position and rucked up her skirt) which struck me like a blow. Now it seems faintly ridiculous, a stock incident of pornography: but I know what I saw and I know how it affected me. I didn't care any more about how she spoke. I wanted only to be alone with her, to touch that white flesh gently, to explore the dark mystery above. I thought of her as being unattainable no longer, she had left the dream world. I didn't devise any elaborate plans for her seduction, didn't even think in terms of seduction. The idea of marriage, then as later, was never further from my head. I had too much to do, too far to go, to take on that burden.

Looking at her dark head bent over the typewriter I was filled with joy and gratitude. The room was very warm; I more than ever noticed the smell of young female flesh and face powder and lipstick and scent. I could hear above the irregular clatter of typewriter keys the regular pounding of the waves. Now and again the wind rattled the windows; I felt the responsibility to record the moment, realizing that it deserved recording, that I should be failing in my duty if I didn't make notes of every detail, that if I didn't record it, it would be as if it had never existed. As Miranda often said to me, my own life, however humdrum it might appear, was all I'd really got for material, I couldn't afford to miss anything, I always had to be on the job. 'On the job,' she'd repeat. 'You know the colloquial meaning of that? Copulation. You've got to have that kind of feeling for everything around you. If the world you live in doesn't make you feel like that all the time, then there's nothing wrong with the world. There's something wrong with you. Later you can slow down awhile, you can remember, you can build. But in the meantime, love, get stuck in.'

Why didn't *she* remember and build? Even at eighteen I asked myself this, always with a sense of disloyalty. Harvey, when once I mentioned it to him, cited the precedent of E. M. Forster. But that to me seemed simple enough: merely lack of creative vitality and the absence of any financial necessity. I doubt if I put it quite as coherently then; I was only aware that I found Forster unreadable. And I might as well be honest: I still do.

Miranda's third novel, though, whatever its technical faults, had vitality. She was, as she herself would put it, still in business. Why hadn't she taken her own advice? I am almost sure now that, young and inexperienced though I was, I could somehow or other have badgered her into writing another novel. Sometimes, I even think that I might with advantage to both of us have played out the rôle of the wild young writer, have been less the model pupil, less the obedient son, have, even at the risk of the destruction of our special relationship, have put my hand up Teacher's skirts, have made a determined pass at Mama.

Once she knew that I had a talent, I could have given her a rougher ride, have not behaved so well, have in fact behaved very badly. I have a notion that that is what she may have expected, have been prepared to forgive, even to indulge. For certainly she had in her London period indulged more than one young writer, sometimes even young writers without the excuse of talent. Maybe that's why she called me a cold bugger.

What disturbs me is that if I had become her lover it might well have provided her with the stimulus that she needed. I'm not at all certain that it would have been good for me. The man-of-the-world always approves of young men being sexually initiated by older women; my father would have been very happy if I'd confirmed his suspicion that Miranda was, as he put it, doing something for me. But Colette, who, to put it mildly, knew more about sex than my father, has said the last word on the older woman-young man relationship. It destroys the young man. He's been given more than he can cope with. Any affair, even the most idyllic, is a battle; but in this battle the woman has too much on her side – too much experience, too much of that terrible self-sufficiency which even the most innocent virgin possesses. A novel is a bundle of messages; one of the messages of my first novel was that the hero didn't win the battle, that although his mistress was dead, he'd never be able to get her out of his system, that what he had from her would spoil him for any other woman.

So Cora was best for me, she wouldn't draw me into an adult relationship before my time. She wasn't my mother and she wasn't my teacher; we were both in every sense of the word still learning. I wasn't in love with her, and I don't think that I ever deluded myself that I was. What I felt was purely physical and none the worse for that. It couldn't be compared with what Maurice felt for Maureen. With those two there was an alliance, a comradeship, they were on each other's side against the world.

But there is always something to be paid. If I could have found a girl who would have been to me what Maureen was to Maurice, I wouldn't have had energy to spare for her and my writing and she wouldn't have permitted my involvement with Miranda and Miranda's Gang.

I didn't, in short, see Cora as a person at all. I might feel guilty about this but for the fact that she didn't see me as a person either, but as the nice rather shy boy who waylaid her in the corridor going out of class and, stammering and blushing a little, asked her to go to the pictures with him on Friday night.

She hesitated for a minute, then said, 'I don't mind.'

I knew then that there couldn't be anything permanent between us, because through Miranda's Gang I'd picked up unconsciously the middle-class convention that if anyone addresses you, particularly if they're issuing an invitation, you smile. Her face had remained without expression. And I'd also picked up the middle-class detestation of the phrase *I don't mind*. But there remained the dark hair and pale face and grey-blue eyes and fine dark eyebrows, there remained her smell of powder and lipstick and, that evening, violets, there remained her scarlet headscarf carried in one long thin hand, there remained the certainty that under her clothes was the dark wonderful mystery. I arranged the details and the others swirled chattering around her again; I walked off quickly along Main Street down to the Coble.

I stopped beside the seawall for a moment and took a deep breath. It was very quiet in the little square; this was the period when TV was beginning to take people out of the streets. I saw Harvey Abington's Morris Eight; I wasn't quite sure whether I wanted to see him in my present mood. Or indeed any of the Gang: what I really wanted to do was to weave fantasies around Cora. And if Jane Badingham was there, as she was almost bound to be, I might become discontented with the fantasies, envious of Harvey. I wove fantasies around Jane too; but they weren't silent. There was something else on my mind; until now I'd shown Miranda each article as I'd written it. I had finished one the day before and was now plucking up courage to send it without showing it to her first.

But as I entered the Coble I put Cora and the article out of my mind and Jane and I went into my favourite fantasy, sitting in a Paris bistro, glasses of absinthe in front of us.

Well, we've done it now. God, what'll they be saying in Engelsea?

I don't care.

Poor old Harvey. He can't understand, can he, that there's such a thing as a coup de foudre?

The Party doesn't acknowledge such decadent bourgeois emotions.

You're a bastard, aren't you? I saw this coming, you know. The very first time I saw you –

I put aside the fantasy as I saw her sitting beside Ted Lewis and gave way to simple longing. She was wearing a plain jersey dress in leaf-brown, the same shade as her hair; it subdued her slight plumpness into a trim voluptuousness.

122

She smiled at me.

'Hi, I loved that piece of yours in the *Statesman*.'

I found myself blushing. I didn't know what to say to her. 'Thank you,' I mumbled. Harvey was talking to Miranda, Ted Lewis was talking to Jack Barrington, Bill Abercorn was sitting a little apart from the rest, his eyes glazed. To cover my confusion, I gave them a half-wave of greeting which they automatically acknowledged.

'You're shy,' she said. 'You really are shy.'

'I expect I'm a bit afraid of you.'

She laughed. She had a pleasant throaty laugh, rather like Miranda's. 'Darling, I wouldn't do you any harm. I wish to God that that bastard Harvey was a bit more afraid of me. He's always telling me what a stupid bourgeois bitch I am.'

'I wouldn't call you names if I were engaged to you. I'd just tell you how pretty you were.'

My hunting instinct had conquered my awkwardness.

'You're not so shy, are you? But I am a stupid bourgeois bitch, I am really. All that stuff about economic determinism and dialectical materialism just bores me stiff.'

'It does me too.'

'Even Miranda's rather keen on it, though she pretends not to be.' She lowered her voice. 'When she's really pissed she goes on about her class being doomed and the triumph of the proletariat. Fuck the proletariat, I say.'

'I'm with you there.'

'Are you really?' She seemed genuinely surprised. Like most middle-class intellectuals she was completely unaware of how obsessively the shopkeeper class, though its whole mode of living may be working-class, disassociates itself from the working class.

'I haven't any class,' I said. It was important, I felt, that

I should get this right. 'I haven't any politics. I haven't the time.'

'You don't think that that's not a bit selfish?'

'I don't care about anything except writing.'

'I don't believe you do.' She nodded in the direction of Jack Barrington. 'You know what his novel's going to be about? The horror of war. He's all het up about war, you see. And he's mad after some chit at his office who won't give him the time of day.'

'I haven't seen the novel,' I said.

'You won't.'

'It isn't finished, is it?'

I hoped that it wouldn't be; I could put up with Harvey writing literary and political articles, and with Bill attempting to write a play, but I couldn't have borne the envy if Jack had actually finished a novel and it was publishable.

'No.' She lowered her voice again. 'Cheer up,' she said, seeming to read my thoughts. 'I doubt that it ever will be. Miranda thinks not, but don't for Christ's sake tell her I told you. Or him either.'

'What are you two whispering about?' Harvey said, coming over to us.

'He's trying to persuade me to come on a dirty weekend with him,' Jane said.

'Precocious little bastard,' Harvey said. He pressed the bell behind me, and squeezed in next to Jane. 'Did you tell him how much we liked his last *Statesman* piece?'

'I told him how much *I* liked it,' Jane said. 'I didn't think it was political enough for you.'

'He's only young,' Harvey said. 'Give him a few more years.'

The barman minced in; Harvey grinned at him. 'How are you, love?'

'The old trotters are killing me,' the barman said. I noticed him look round the room, searching the face of each man in turn, returning to Harvey; I noticed too the way the full mouth turned down a little at the corners.

'You shouldn't wear tight shoes,' Harvey said.

The barman's feet were very small, made to appear still smaller by pointed glossy tan shoes. 'You have to suffer to be beautiful,' he said. 'What would you like me to get you, sir?' He was on the defensive now.

'Four pints of bitter and three halves,' Harvey said. 'And one for yourself.'

'Ta ever so,' the barman said. He minced out, leaving a cloud of perfume behind him.

'Poor sod,' Harvey said. 'I wonder how he ended up here?'

'You'd better ask him,' Jane said.

'I might at that,' Harvey said. He was exuding self-satisfaction. He turned to me. 'I wonder that you haven't thought of taking a degree.'

'I haven't got Matric.'

'There are ways round that,' he said.

'I want to be a journalist.'

'Having a degree doesn't prevent you from being a journalist. God, if only you saw the gibbering illiterates they let into universities these days – '

Miranda looked over at me. 'I want a word with you, ducky.'

'Excuse me,' I said to Harvey. He pulled a face. I sat down beside Miranda.

'It's a month since you've shown me anything. What's the matter?'

'I'm stuck. And I've been busy.'

'What with?'

'Shorthand.'

'That's nothing. At your age half an hour's practice a day is enough. You're not getting lazy, are you?'

'I like to read too,' I said.

'Honey, it's now or never. You either work like stink now or you laze and get nowhere. Show me that article. Bring it over to my house tomorrow night. Everybody gets stuck from time to time.'

I had been going to send the article and say nothing to her; I wanted to do this one on my own. But she was too strong for me, the habit of obedience was not to be shaken off.

'All right,' I said. 'About nine.'

'About nine. What was Harvey talking to you about?'

'Taking a degree.'

'That's really very naughty of him. It'd be the worst thing in the world for you.' She grinned. 'It'd serve him right if you seduced Jane. You two seemed very thick.'

'You don't miss much,' I said.

'Early training, my poppet. And natural female nosiness. All novelists are gossips and scandalmongers really. That's why I want you to stay here a bit longer. I'm not sure that I shouldn't try to get you a job on the *Clarion*. Except that I'm not terribly well in with the editor.'

'It's an awful paper.'

'It makes a profit, ducky. It exists to cram as many names in as possible, which boosts circulation, which boosts advertisements. It really would be good training for you. A damned sight better than listening to tripe about Beowulf and the Ancren Riwle and the Lake Poets. Hemingway and O'Hara began as journalists. It'll make you or break you.'

'I'm getting a bit fed up of reportage,' I said. 'I want to write some stories.'

'Oh God, no! *Read* them if you want, don't try to write them. There's almost no market for them, love, it's a waste of time.'

She was right, of course. Even then there were a few places where the sort of short story that I'd be likely to write would be published; but I wanted to create character, to write dialogue, to devise situations, I wanted to do something more than describe.

'Hemingway and O'Hara wrote stories,' I said.

'Because there was a market for them, you dope. It isn't there now. It's not your length anyway, and think yourself damn lucky.'

'How do you know?' I'd never felt rebellious before; probably sexual frustration had stirred it up.

'I couldn't tell you. Except I think that you want to go *into* things, you can't just look at them from one angle. That awful story you showed me – it was the beginning of something, not the beginning and end.'

'I could write a novel then,' I said sulkily. Even though I knew that the story was awful I didn't like hearing it being described as such.

'Perhaps you could. And there'd be only one fate worse for you than having it rejected. That'd be having it published. You'd be a freak.'

'I'd take the chance.'

She laughed. 'Oh, it'd be marvellous, wouldn't it? A real writer at eighteen! I bet you're already seeing the reviews in your mind's eye. It'd be absolutely bang on, wouldn't it? You'd go to London then and they'd make a great fuss of you. For a while. Until the next freak came along. And then the invitations would dry up. And the money too. And what would you write about? Because you'd have used up everything in your first novel.'

'It needn't be like that for me.'

'Tom, no-one ever thinks it's going to be like that for them. They always think that it's going to be different for them. And it never is. Christ, isn't that what literature is all about? Here's the rocks and the swamps and here's the path – and we get stuck in the swamps, we cut our feet to bits on the rocks. We think that it'll be different for us. It isn't, it isn't . . . Do you understand?'

I nodded.

'You don't,' she said bitterly. 'But you've got something, otherwise why should I bother? What the hell are you fed up about, anyway? You're getting published, and you're getting paid.'

'I'm just a bit fed up,' I said. That was an understatement; suddenly a mood of absolute despair had overtaken me.

'I think you really are,' she said. She glanced at Jane, who now was talking to Harvey, and she smiled. 'I've a shrewd idea why. Well, you won't get anything in this world if you don't try for it.'

'No use in trying.' I wasn't six feet tall with a war wound, I wasn't twenty-eight, I didn't have a good job, I didn't have an officer's accent, I wasn't engaged to her. At that moment another part of my first novel fell into place; I was feeling much the same as my hero looking at the rich and handsome and self-assured young man who seems to have taken possession of the girl he, the hero, wants.

'Isn't it?' Her voice had sunk very low. 'You're not bad-looking, Tom. No woman objects to being desired.' She moistened her lips. 'You know what the secret of sexual success is? Have a bash, go ahead, try your luck. It should be very interesting.'

My depression was replaced by an overmastering excitement, seeing Jane naked in my arms. But at the same time there was a vague disquiet; there was something about the way in which Miranda had pronounced the word *interesting* that I hadn't liked. Now I can see what she was doing. Out of love of mischief and out of a sort of debased creative instinct, she was deliberately interfering with three people's lives. She knew that despite my momentary rebellion her suggestions were commands to me, knew also that the idea of making love to Jane had to be brought out before I'd do anything about it. She wanted to see what would happen; she intended to use real people to divert herself, in much the same way that the Romans used condemned criminals to be murdered and tortured in real earnest on the stage.

If she'd still been writing, I believe that she wouldn't have made the suggestion: it would have been enough to have been furnished with the ingredients for a dramatic situation. Perhaps I make too much of this, searching as I do now for reasons for her long abstention from writing. I only know that from that evening onwards I no longer saw Jane as unattainable and that there seemed a change in her attitude towards me. But let me be honest; whatever Miranda's motives I was grateful to her. I regret no part of our relationship and what happened to me that evening least of all.

Ten

It was raining hard on the evening I met Cora at the Rialto Cinema on Main Street just opposite the square where the Coble stood. I arrived a few minutes early and stood in the shelter of the marquee in my trench coat and grey trilby which had a narrow brim and was high in front and sloped down sharply. And there's another thing to be grateful for; waiting outside the cinema on a rainy night drawing deeply at my cigarette, the hat well over my eyes and my trenchcoat collar turned up, I was Humphrey Bogart, I was Dick Powell, I was, above all, Jimmy Cagney, I was menace and doom and mystery and masculinity and there was too the minor but solid pleasure of possessing garments that protected one against the elements.

The Rialto, now a bingo parlour, was a small cinema in the same style as the adjoining terrace houses but standing a little higher, with a narrow passageway to the left and a road to the right leading to the car park behind. TV hadn't yet made really serious inroads into cinema audiences, Hollywood was still a going concern and (though this may be merely my imagination working in retrospect) the building had about it the air of being the outpost of a great empire, one was conscious of a link which somehow connected with that empire. I don't have that feeling now even in West End cinemas during a hit, I'm not sure as I was sure every time I visited the Rialto, that escape into a different world is guaranteed.

Cora was only a few minutes late, but it was long enough for me to foresee that I was going to be stood up, that I was going to be made a fool of. But when she came up to me in a white raincoat, and white pixie hood smelling of rain and lavender, that was something to add to the total of things I'm grateful for.

'I'm frightfully sorry I'm late,' she said. *Frightfully* was a word made to order for her accent; she drew it out with relish.

'I've only just arrived,' I said, and took her arm. We went into the warm darkness and the smell of rose disinfectant, going upstairs to the balcony between rows of pastel tinted photos of stars, some of whom are still around, some of whom reappear now briefly, dead of an overdose of sleeping tablets, bankrupted in some shady enterprise, charged with the possession of drugs or the corruption of minors, attempting comebacks in plays which never reach the West End and, now and again, acting the pants off everybody in small parts in a feature film.

The cinema wasn't as full as it normally was on a wet Friday evening, but there were enough people there to bring the film to life. A film needs an audience as much as a play does: a small audience spoils the best film, a big audience makes a bad one bearable. The film was *The Pride of St Louis* and even now when old American films are trendy no-one is going to remember it. But it told a story, the background was authentic, and it had the high professional gloss that only Hollywood has achieved. And that is something to be grateful for again. Holding hands in a rather scruffy little cinema watching a film not of the first rank to say the least of it, I was entirely happy. Her hands were small and slim and cool: and that, for the duration of the film, was enough. I had some Rowntree's fruit pastilles with me and, whenever I passed her one, would make it an excuse to lean closer and brush her cheek with mine. The difference between the smooth softness of a woman's cheek and mine seemed incredibly exciting and still does. I had of course her breasts and what was between her legs still very much in my mind; but in the meantime I was in no hurry.

When we emerged from the cinema it had stopped raining. The air's always as if washed clean after rain, but the smell of salt and seaweed and the contrast with the disinfectant and tobacco scented atmosphere of the cinema added up to a full sixty seconds during which I was conscious of some enormous promise having been honoured, of an angry lion suddenly tame and nuzzling my hand like a dog.

'It's smashing now,' I said to Cora.

She took my arm. 'It's a little chilly,' she said. 'But very nice and fresh.'

'Would you like a drink?'

'I wouldn't mind.'

The phrase irritated me, as always, and depression briefly replaced elation. My body wanted her body and I knew from the way in which she nestled against me for warmth that her body didn't object to mine. But my mind had reached out to hers and found nothing there that I wanted. I looked over at the Coble, then turned down Main Street.

'I thought we might go to the Cochrane.'

'The Lounge is very nice.'

'Did you like the film?'

'I cried a bit in the end when he went out to play with those kiddies. I thought that that was ever so clever, didn't you?'

'It worked.'

'You're a funny boy,' she said.

'How am I funny?'

'Sometimes you seem ever so grown-up. Then you seem just a kid. In that funny hat – ' She suddenly snatched my hat from me and ran away down the street laughing. I ran after her and caught up with her as she went down a side-street and then down an alleyway. She stood panting, holding the hat behind her.

'Give me it,' I said.

She shook her head. Her pixie hood had come loose; I could smell her hair, warm and clean. I kissed her. There are not many events which are as good in realization as in anticipation, but this was one of them. I wasn't Daphnis and I don't suppose that she was Chloë, but there was something innocent about our first kiss that I've never forgotten. I stroked her hair and held her for a moment.

'You're beautiful,' I said.

She smiled. We might have gone on from there but we heard footsteps coming down the street and she moved away from me.

'It's getting late if you want a drink.'

'I'm not bothered.'

'Silly boy,' she said. 'Come on.'

We walked along the Main Street; she swung my hat in her hand. 'I'll throw it in the sea.'

'It cost me a lot of money.'

'I don't care. Promise me, you'll never wear it again.'

'What if it rains?'

'You're not sugar, you won't melt.'

She wasn't attempting to speak Standard English any longer; even the quality of her voice became more pleasant as she ceased to push it out of its natural range. I began to wish that I'd taken her into the Coble. And then as we went into the Lounge of the Lord Cochrane, among the ships in bottles and steering wheels and ship pictures and harpoons and oak panels and mullioned windows and the smell of cigars, I seemed to see a change take place in her. The Cochrane Lounge was the chief, in fact the only place where the middle class of Engelsea and district gathered: both Cora and I noted for our different reasons in our different ways the preponderance of tweed and mink and camelhair and Chanel and sheepskin and gold watches and large diamond rings and the plum-in-the-mouth accent. My hat more than ever looked out of place, even when carried; I saw, or imagined that I saw, looks of amused contempt on the faces around me.

I helped Cora off with her coat and hastily took off mine. There were two empty seats at a large table nearby; I showed Cora into one and put down the coats and hat on the other, covering the hat with the trenchcoat. That seemed wrong too; the middle-class fashion at that time was for light, almost white riding-coats with red linings.

'What would you like to sup, love?' I asked Cora. *Sup* wasn't the word I'd have used normally, but if I couldn't be like the others it was better to be as different as possible.

'Oh,' she said, drawing the monosyllable out, 'a Bloody Mary would be nice.'

At the bar I found myself invisible; almost literally so, since all the men there were at least a head taller than me. The two barmaids evidently knew all the customers at the bar; their smile switched off when their eyes were in my direction, then switched on again when they went away from me. I kept my temper by reminding myself that it wouldn't be of any avail for me to lose it and by making notes for an article which would subtly portray the bar-maids and the customers as posturing, affected, toadying and toadied-to idiots.

I think that I was served when the look on my face indicated that I was too interested in my own thoughts to care; I bought myself a Scotch, though I would rather have had a pint.

I put the coats and the hat on my knees when I sat down; it was rather awkward, and no-one else seemed to have the same problem.

I offered Cora a cigarette which, rather to my surprise, she accepted. She had refused one in the cinema. I remember that I had a Perspex cigarette case which popped up cigarettes one at a time; I longed for a silver or gold one that evening but I never was to be able to afford one until they went out of fashion. I don't know why they went out of fashion, any more than I know why the habit of tapping the end of the cigarette before lighting it went out of fashion; nor do I know why this seems so important now.

'You look *frightfully* serious,' Cora said. 'All the cares of the world on your shoulders. Someone said you write for the magazines. I expect you're terribly clever.'

'Not very clever and not very serious,' I said. Her re-fined accent had returned and she was speaking very loudly and with a determined brightness.

'Do they pay you for it?'

'Of course.'

'I've seen you passing the shop sometimes,' she said. 'You look miles away. Then you look at the window and scowl.' She giggled. To my consternation I found myself blushing.

'I've got to look somewhere.'

'Oh, you're not the only one. Our window seems very boring to me.'

Suddenly I had an excruciating spasm of lust and was grateful for the coats across my knees. My foreskin had caught in something; at the same time I had a mental picture of Cora in her underwear which wouldn't go away.

'I'll explain it all to you some day,' I said.

'You needn't bother. I think you're rather hot on the q.t., aren't you?'

'Don't you trust me?'

'My mother says trust no man, even the parson.'

I stroked her hand. 'You can trust me.'

'You go with that Miranda Abberwick's lot, don't you?'

'Sometimes,' I said.

'My mother said she's a bad influence. There's a young man from our street – Jim Camarthen, he's a cousin of mine – he had a good job at the Town Hall. He used to write poetry – silly stuff. I couldn't understand it. Mrs Abberwick encouraged him – '

'Is that bad?'

'He threw up his job to go to London.'

'So what?' I'd never heard Miranda or anyone in the Gang refer to Jim Camarthen; I felt angry and jealous, but tried to keep my tone neutral.

'He was had up in Court, that's what. Lucky not to go to jail.'

'What did he do?'

She lowered her voice. 'Went with a girl under age.'

'Depends on the girl.'

'Oh, she looked older than fourteen. The judge said so.'

'You can't blame Miranda for that anyway.'

'His mother does. Says he changed completely when he started going around with Miranda's lot, he wasn't the same lad – boy – any more.'

'I haven't heard of him.'

'I bet you haven't. He doesn't come home any more. Ashamed to show his face.'

'Who cares? He's not the only one, is he?'

'His mother cares. The Camarthens are big Methodists, you know. Look down on us because we don't go to chapel.'

'Miranda's always been decent to me,' I said. 'Jim Camarthen would probably have gone to London anyway.'

What really bothered me was that I hadn't ever seen any of Jim Camarthen's poetry. It didn't seem a very good omen for me. If one of her swans was a goose, another could be.

'You don't look very pleased,' she said.

'I couldn't care less.' But I couldn't care more; it had spoilt my whole evening. It meant that I couldn't trust Miranda again. I'd associated her with success and now I associated her with failure.

'It's your own business,' she said. 'I just thought I'd tell you.'

'I wish you hadn't,' I said. I looked away from her across the room and saw Ralph Thoralby and Ted Lewis. They were arguing in low voices. Then I noticed tears in Ralph's eyes but put it down to the smoky atmosphere which seemed actually to have become thicker since we'd come in. Ted turned away from Ralph and saw me. He waved, and nudged Ralph, who waved too. They came over to our table.

'I was going to ask you why you weren't at the Coble,' Ralph said. 'But it'd be a silly question.' He smiled at Cora.

'Cora Ramelton,' I said. 'Ralph Thoralby, Ted Lewis.'

'Pleased to meet you,' she said; Ted looked vaguely contemptuous but Ralph continued to smile.

137

'Pleased to meet *you*, my dear,' he said. 'What good taste you have, Tom.' He looked at his watch. 'We've just time for a quick one at the Coble,' he said. 'Cheerio, Tom. Cheerio, Cora.'

Ted said nothing, but as he followed Ralph out started arguing with him again.

'He's nice, the older one,' Cora said. 'He speaks beautifully.' She sounded rather wistful; perhaps for a moment she was comparing her accent with the genuine article.

'He was right about my having good taste,' I said. 'You're lovely, really you are. You're the best-looking girl in the room. By a long chalk.'

'You say that to all the girls.'

'I've never said it to any girl before,' I said. It occurred to me that I was speaking the absolute truth. And what I kept detecting on the faces of the men around me was envy. It didn't matter about my trenchcoat and awful hat, or that I didn't have a car; I had something which they all wanted. This isn't the sort of feeling that any decent chap would admit to, but I've never pretended to be a decent chap. Half the pleasure I derived from Cora was from being seen with her.

Looking back, I can't imagine what she saw in me. It wasn't that she was particularly impressed by my writing, although she was curious about how much I was paid for it. It's more likely that she thought of me as the heir to a flourishing small business and as a Knossington with all sorts of useful connections. I'm sure that she didn't want to be a fisherman's wife, just as I'm sure that she had social ambitions. The shorthand and typing classes were one means of rising; I believe that she had a vision of herself as the secretary who marries her boss. If I'd been her I wouldn't have wasted my time with Tom Metfield, but contrived to put myself in the way of meeting young men of the boss class; I would have seen how valuable an asset my looks were.

I don't think that she really did. At least, not consistently. Part of her was searching for a rich husband, part of her was searching simply for a man to love her. And I don't think that she wanted to leave Engelsea. Most people don't want to leave their home town, particularly when their families – she belonged to one of the two main fishing families in Engelsea – have close links with the place.

But I over-complicate matters. The fact is, I see now, that she fancied me. She needn't be ashamed to bring me home to tea, I'd always be able to support her, and I had no connection with the sea, about which she knew Kipling was right. It was the old grey widow-maker; that was a quotation which I heard her use more than once.

Perhaps too she smelled success on me; the most unsophisticated of women are better at this than men. But I'm being unfair; though obviously she had aspirations towards a higher status, I don't think that she was a calculating sort of person.

None of this has very much to do with what followed during the next few months, at first in the Victoria Park, a large hilly stretch of land north-east of the Promenade, but for the most part in the living-room at home. It could be bitterly cold in Engelsea in winter, but very few people used the park, and there was an abundance of shelters and trees, mostly conifers. At home we always kept a roaring fire – there was nothing mean about my father and Hetty – but though they never returned until late, and never unexpectedly, I never felt quite certain that Amelia or Lester wouldn't come downstairs. The hero of my first novel of course had no such problems; the children in the house where he went baby-sitting with the rich man's daughter never stirred, and the older woman borrowed a friend's flat.

In the sex manuals I used to read at that period it was always pointed out how reprehensible and unsatisfying petting was and how there was a grave danger of it making the real thing disappointing. It wasn't like that with me. I've pushed a great deal of what happened in my youth to the back of my mind, but I've never let go of any detail of what happened between Cora and me.

It still was – in that part of England at least – a restrictive society sexually. The general assumption was that unmarried people shouldn't copulate. I don't in the least care whether this was a good or a bad thing in itself: the effect on me was to heighten sensuality, to make the most trivial and fleeting contacts with the opposite sex almost unbearably exciting. Naturally I wanted the real thing, but every successive intimacy was complete in itself, something to be grateful for, something to be treasured. What I learned from Cora has stayed with me; I've never ceased to be grateful for women and the amazing and wonderful difference between them and us.

I don't very clearly remember the interior of her home; the exterior was almost a duplicate of ours except that along the tops of the terrace ran an absurd little crenellated parapet. There was a great deal of new-looking furniture and a great many ornaments and pictures and photos and a large shiny radiogram but no TV. The mother was a small thin woman who talked very rapidly and always wore an apron; the father was a large dour man with a big jaw and very hard hands. I had tea there three or four times, and Cora had tea at my house three or four times. I've tried to remember these occasions but my usually reliable memory comes up with only a few snatches of conversation. I don't think that Cora's parents liked me very much; they probably felt that their only daughter could have done better for herself, and I don't blame them. My father and Hetty, on the other hand, didn't seem to care very much; Hetty praised her looks and laughed at her accent and my father would ask me if I'd got it in yet.

Cora said nothing about marriage, but I felt that I was going out with her under false pretences. It didn't weigh on me overmuch: I have never had a very active sense of guilt. But once I saw what turn her mind was taking I should have been honest with her.

I wasn't in love with her. She was kind and uncomplicated and even-tempered and I liked her, and that was as far as it went. It was her body that I loved, and gradually came to know as well as my own. The most important thing I was to learn from her was something which before I only knew in theory: that women enjoy sex as much as men.

The first time we went to Victoria Park was one cold November night. We entered the park from a path at the side and walked along between the pines hand-in-hand. There was a full moon and the trees looked black rather than green; it was very quiet in the park, and the crunch of our feet on the loose gravel seemed unnaturally loud. I was so excited that I found it hard to speak; she didn't speak but her face was serene and faintly smiling.

The path climbed steeply upwards; at the top was a large wooden shelter.

'Let's sit down and have a cigarette,' I said hoarsely.

'I don't mind if I do.'

I offered her a cigarette. 'What a cute little case,' she said.

'You've seen it before.'

I wondered what exactly she expected me to do this evening, whether she was hot stuff, all for it, whether she'd be able to tell that I was a virgin and, almost simultaneously, whether she'd smack my face if I tried.

We sat smoking for a while. I tried to blow smoke rings but the breeze through a broken pane prevented them from forming.

'It's nice here,' she said. 'About the only hill in the district.'

'I dreamed about you last night,' I said. I had actually dreamed about being lost in London with someone pursuing me whose face I couldn't see, but how would she know?

'Was it a nice dream?'

'Very nice.'

'How nice?'

'I daren't tell you.'

'Naughty,' she said, and gave me a little dig in the ribs. 'You're a dreamy sort of boy, aren't you?'

'I think about real things.'

'Such as?'

'Everything. And what goes on inside people's heads.'

She threw her cigarette on the floor and put her foot on it and snatched mine from my mouth. She moved closer to me and tilted up her face. 'You're really quite shy, aren't you?' she whispered.

She kissed with her mouth open and her tongue searching for mine. After a while I unfastened her topcoat and took off my own. I ran my hand down her back feeling the outline of her slip and bra straps and the contrast in texture between wool and nylon.

I suppose it was then that my taste in women was fixed. I haven't ever consciously limited myself to one type, but when I look back most of the women in my life have been slim and dark with a tendency to domineer. I didn't know this then, all my senses being in an uproar of delight, but I've realized it since. She really took charge that evening, and continued in charge. Hoping she would stop me and hoping she wouldn't, I unbuttoned the top of her dress and felt her shudder. I put my hand under her bra, which was very tight. She reached up behind her, her lips still on mine, and did something; her breasts swung forward into my hands.

It was different from what I'd expected; the few nude photos I'd seen were so posed as to make the breasts seem as if held by an invisible brassiere, and the nipples were somehow minimized. Looking down at hers in the moonlight I was for a second almost frightened; the nipples and the rings round them were so large and, though small, they dropped a little with their own weight. I put my head on them. 'Baby,' she said. 'Baby,' and pressed my head down on them.

That was as far as it went that evening and as far as it was to go the next five times we were alone together. In the back of my head I had some idea of a gradual seduction: in the event I let my instincts lead me. Each time what I had satisfied me but not to satiation, and I would keep remembering it after, and all my perceptions – the smell of the sea, the texture of wood and cloth, the taste of apples in particular – were transformed, were both stronger and more delicate.

I've made a mess of my marriage and if I marry Deirdre I expect I'll make a mess of that. And of course I was to make a mess of my relationship with Cora. I'm obviously not good husband material and I won't go down in history as a great lover either. But with Cora I learned the beginning and the end of wisdom in love, which is to take it easy, to do what you want to do, not what you imagine is expected of you, not what the manuals sent under plain cover recommend. For what you want will in the end be what the woman wants, just as long as you're not trying to prove anything.

I always knew this though I couldn't then articulate it, and Cora must have done too. And it must have helped that I'd grown away from all the boys I'd gone to school with. There was no-one of my own age to talk to about Cora, to boast to about the successive stages of our intimacy. The end of that is a feeling of betrayal, the presence of invisible spectators egging one on to a kind of gang-rape. I gave the hero of my first novel a best friend with whom he compared notes on his sexual progress but – I've been saying this unavailingly ever since it was published – he wasn't me. He was rather more of the predator, the hunter: I in my way have always been Eros's adoring servant.

A price had to be paid for all this: I began to neglect my writing. I even tried to write poetry; Cora liked it, though I suspect that she didn't understand it and would rather that it had rhymed. It had a few merits: I knew enough to avoid adjectives and clichés and now and again would come up with a phrase which would come near to expressing what I felt.

On one of my now rare visits to the Coble I gave some of the poems to Miranda. She said nothing at the time but a week later 'phoned me.

'Come to my house tonight. About seven.'

'I'm not absolutely sure – '

'I am, ducky. I've spent a lot of time on you and I'm not going to see it wasted.'

She hung up. My father glanced at me over his paper. 'She's a right bossy-boots, that one.'

'She's helped me a lot.'

'Very kind of her. Used to know a widow when I was your age. She helped me too.'

'It isn't like that,' I said irritated.

'Wish it were. You're seeing a lot of that Cora these days.'

'What's wrong with her?'

'Nothing. She's a nice lass. But I know more about you than you think. Chaps like your cousin Maurice – it suits them to be tied down early. But it won't suit you.'

'I'm not going to be tied down.'

'You'd better be bloody careful then, otherwise you'll be arse-over-tail into a right hornets' nest. You haven't mentioned marriage to her, have you?'

I shook my head.

'She will, you'll see.'

'How do you know?'

'Because I've been young myself, you silly bugger.' He picked up his paper, then put it down again. 'Listen. You get into any trouble, you tell me. But why wait till then? You'd better go away now.'

'You're throwing me out?'

'Bloody thickhead! Of course I'm not. I'm thinking of what's best for you.'

'What about the shop?'

'Oh, I'll contrive to run it without you.'

'I'll think about it.'

'Please your bloody self.' He picked up his paper again. He wasn't a man to waste words. If he'd been more persistent, if I'd been more communicative, then my life might have been very different. Certainly my first novel would have had a different plot: for it was at this moment that its shape was decided.

Eleven

When I rang the doorbell of the Grange at seven that
evening there was no sound. I knocked at the door which
stood a little ajar. The light was on in the hall, but the
drawing-room and Max's den were dark. I knocked loudly
for some ten minutes, beginning to feel rather foolish.
Had I misunderstood her? The conversation with my
father had depressed me with its intimations of trouble
ahead, and I'd glanced at a half-finished article before
I'd set out and come to the conclusion that it would have
to be rewritten. And this was the image of failure: a cold
damp night, a large dark house, and knocking to no avail.

Miranda came to the door, frowning. 'Why the hell
didn't you just come in?' she asked. 'Why do you think
I left the bloody door ajar?'

'I'm sorry,' I said.

'Oh, I'm in a foul temper. That damned doorbell – it's
supposed to have been repaired. Sod and rot the bloody
working classes! You, too, mate!'

'What have I done?'

She showed me into her study, a room at the back of
the house which originally had been the breakfast-room.
It was the sort of room which I should have liked for my-

self with the two bookcases running almost from floor to ceiling and the huge desk at the window; it was large enough to have space for everything needed for writing and small enough to be cosy. There were two coffee tables, a large leather-covered sofa, and two large matching armchairs; I can't remember any ornaments or pictures except for the small photograph of her two sons in school uniform, dark-haired and smiling, on her desk, and the large painting above the fireplace of herself when young in a white evening dress. The fitted carpet was cream and thick and the walls were almost of the same colour; it was both luxurious and austere and almost unnaturally tidy. With the fire in the large tiled fireplace roaring up the chimney and the central heating turned up high, it was too warm for comfort: I now wore a belt and before sitting in the chair which Miranda indicated to me took off my jacket without being asked.

Miranda took out the sheaf of poems from the desk. She pointed to the bottle of Haig on the table. 'Help yourself. And pour me one.'

She sat down on the other chair looking at the poems. I moved the other coffee table to her right side and put down her drink on it. I knew now exactly the size of drink she liked.

There was a long silence. I asked myself why I never felt comfortable in the room and decided that the answer was that it was a workroom in which no work had ever been done, but that when the shelves and desk had been put in she had every confidence of doing good work there. The silence stretched itself out irritatingly; I didn't like the sensation of being under judgement.

'What have I done?'
'What?'
'What have I done wrong?'

'You've wasted your time. This stuff is self-indulgent crap. It's *feelings*. What did René say?'

René was the name by which we now always referred to Rilke.

'Poems are not feelings, these we have soon enough – '

'Exactly. Christ, you don't realize how lucky you are, to know that at your age; who cares about your bloody feelings, anyway? What do they all boil down to? You want to screw this girl, bloody good luck to you. But that isn't *writing*.'

'Love's a legitimate subject for the poet.'

'But you're not a poet, dear. This is tum-ti-tum blank verse with an original image thrown in now and again. You just haven't got it, you haven't the ear.'

'I suppose Jim Camarthen has,' I said sulkily. I'd never brought up his name before.

She looked startled. 'Yes. He's not as good a *writer* as you're going to be, but he's a poet and you're not.' She drained her glass and held it out to me; I refilled it.

'Why didn't you tell me about him?'

'You're jealous. You want to be the only pebble on the beach, don't you?'

To my surprise I found tears coming to my eyes. 'You might have told me.'

'Oh, you're typical. You're going to be a real stinker when you grow up. You want all the attention that's going, don't you? You're the only writer in the world, aren't you?' Her tone was surprisingly tender, and amused.

'Yes, I am! Who's Jim Camarthen? Why didn't you tell me?' I knew as I said it that I was behaving childishly, but I couldn't help it.

'The wonder is that no-one told you before. People forget, of course . . . Anyway, why the hell should I tell you?'

'It's not fair,' I muttered.

'Not fair? Darling, I don't give a bugger. I get through my life by avoiding everything that's unpleasant. I'm a champion escapist, I've built my castle and pulled up the drawbridge.'

'What happened to him?'

'Booze. Getting mixed up with Soho layabouts. Just not being tough enough. Might be just a phase. Sometimes going to the bottom is just what a writer needs. Don't look at me like that!'

'Is he still writing?'

'How the hell should I know? I saw something of his in a scrotty little review a chum of mine brought me. But that was ages since . . . I told him not to go until he'd fixed himself up with a decent job, I *told* him and better told him . . .'

'Haven't you seen him at all?'

'I don't want to talk about him any more. It's you I'm concerned with.'

'The new toy.'

She stood up suddenly and came over to me, breathing heavily. 'I ought to hit you, you little bastard. Why do you suppose I bother with you unless it's because you've got something? And I don't want to see it wasted. You're chasing this illiterate slut now and you're going to chase her right up the aisle if you're not careful. Have you fucked her yet? Tell me the truth now.'

I shook my head. She stared at me. 'All right. But it's not for want of trying, is it?'

'It's my business.'

'That's not you speaking. It's your glands. You want to be a writer, any fool can be a husband. That's not for you. Listen, you're not the marrying kind. Do you know how I know? Because I don't think I am. And you're like me.' She ruffled my hair; the gesture was oddly soothing, devoid of any sexual connotation. 'We're always on our tod, aren't we? You see, I manage with old Max because we've come to an agreement. I leave him alone and he leaves me alone as long as I don't do it in the street and frighten the horses. And there's plenty of money. That makes things easy. One day you'll have plenty of money if you do what I tell you. And then you'll be free.'

'I'll not get plenty of money from *Vanguard* and the *Statesman*,' I said.

'You'll write a novel. Not yet, you're not ready for it. You'll write a lot of novels. Every damned thing you dream about you'll have. You're tough enough, and you're cold enough and you can *see*. But don't get entangled with anyone now.'

'It's experience,' I said.

'Then buy some French letters, for God's sake! Don't act out the business of being in love. It isn't for you. It's good enough for ordinary people. It isn't for you. You mustn't eat table d'hôte. It's a good enough menu for the rest of them, but you wait and have what you want. I'll get you the proper sort of job in London when the time comes. Just be patient.'

'I like Cora,' I said obstinately. 'I'm not thinking of marriage.'

'But *she* is, dear.' She held out her empty glass. She was drinking more quickly than ever I'd seen her but was showing no signs of it. 'I know about Cora. Ralph described her to me. I know the type. She's a shopgirl, isn't she? And her father's a fisherman?'

My surprise must have shown on my face. She laughed. 'Yes,' she said mimicking the accent of the Gestapo man in war films, 've have our vays of finding out.'

I poured myself another whisky. 'You're enjoying yourself, aren't you, Miranda?'

'You're very impudent,' she said.

I put her drink into her hand. 'You enjoy arranging other people's lives.'

She sat down. Her cream linen dress was a little shorter than usual and as she crossed her legs I saw what at that age I always automatically looked for. But there was no physical desire: I think that there was a point in the evening when I was at that stage but I had now passed it.

'Yes,' she said. 'I enjoy it. *C'est mon métier*. With people who are worth it. It grows on you, Tom. It's my nearest approach to being involved.'

'Is that so bad? Being involved?'

'The worst thing in the world for writers. Cast a cold eye, On life, on death, Horseman, pass by . . . You've got to cast a cold eye, Tom. If you poke this girl you've got to realize it doesn't mean anything.' She tapped the sheaf of poems. 'You're trying to kid yourself that it'll mean more than that. The act itself means a hell of a lot. It's about time you had a woman, anyway. And it's nice that it should be prettied up a bit, that you should like the person. But don't get involved. The world's full of women, and you'll have your share of them.' She looked at me appraisingly. 'Women will always like you. You like women, and that's rare in this bloody country. Max doesn't like women, you know. Oh, he's not *queer*. In and out and slinks back to his own room, but he wouldn't mess about with a *chap*. He's in London now – old school reunion. Having the hell of a time reliving the best days of his life. I just bet they were too . . . Tell you what, love, I'm rather pissed. Another great pleasure. Got to be careful, though, it plays hell with the complexion . . . When Max is away I generally contrive to get up to some little teeny bit of mischief . . . Don't suppose he'd notice if I did when he was there, but it seems a waste of a golden opportunity if I don't do *something* . . .'

Hemingway padded in and licked her hand. He brought in with him a smell of grass and earth but only the faintest, not unpleasant, doggy smell. 'Sit,' said Miranda, and he subsided suddenly beside the fire. 'You don't have a dog, do you?' she asked. I shook my head. 'It's just as well. You get involved with them too. Sometimes I've just thought of clearing out, going back to London, but he wouldn't be so happy in London.' She grinned, her face suddenly the face of the girl in the picture. 'Well, it's as good an excuse as any . . .' The fine lines returned to her face. 'Jane likes you.'

'Jane?'

'Jane Badingham, you fool.'

'She's engaged.'

'That's nothing to do with it. I may not write any more, but I've a pair of eyes in my head. She's been a wild one in her time. Couldn't you tell?'

'How could I?' I was actually blushing.

'Of course you couldn't. That's why you're not ready to write fiction yet.'

'She's years older than me.'

'That's the attraction, darling. Younger men aren't my cup of tea, but it's different with some women. Not that she's all that much older.'

'Harvey could be a nasty customer,' I said.

She moistened her lips. 'You'd be playing with fire. But it's fun, you know. You'd be surprised how many people are – gamblers. Like those Irishmen who used to wager their heads or their balls when they'd run out of money . . .'

'Like Ralph.'

Her eyebrows shot up. 'You'd noticed?'

'I'm not as stupid as I look.'

'I think Ted's just – rather flattered. No harm in it so far. You know, Ralph still doesn't know which way he's going. At his age – it's ridiculous really. But I have to live here, and I've to consider Max's position to some extent . . .'

'I don't think there's much you can do about it.'

'You say that with some relish. You'd like there to be trouble, wouldn't you?'

'It's all material.' She was quite right: I had nothing against Ralph or Ted, but I would have welcomed the spectacle of disaster, just as professional soldiers welcome war.

'Oh, I'm with you, dear. If we were in London now, I wouldn't lift a finger. But Engelsea's another kettle of fish. Why kettle of fish? Christ, I *am* pissed . . .'

'It's getting late,' I said. I knew that I ought to be observing her in detail: this was how a middle-aged woman got drunk. But another side of me didn't want to watch her, found the spectacle too ugly, felt that to stay would have been a kind of betrayal.

'It isn't getting late, but you had better go. I'll put on a record soon, some nice doomy Wagner, I think, and get all tearful and guilt-laden. And sorry for myself.'

I rose. 'Goodnight, love.' I kissed her forehead: it was very hot.

'Remember, though. No more poetry. And watch your step with Cora.'

But a month later, babysitting one evening, I didn't watch my step, I followed my instincts. Nor did I do anything about Jane: the opportunity never presented itself. Nor did I stop writing poetry: I stopped showing it to Miranda. I did, however, stop writing tum-ti-tum blank verse: on the evening that I didn't watch my step with Cora I found a Petrarchan sonnet assembling itself in my head at the moment I entered her.

'Be careful,' she said: and I found a place for the words in the sonnet at the same time as I reflected that I hadn't ever before in all my reading realized what the phrase meant. I was careful, groaning with pleasure on the floor, the heat of the fire on my loins, my face on her bare breasts; the pleasure stopped but the sonnet continued.

'I love you,' she said.

'I love you,' I said automatically, and decided not to put that in the sonnet; there was no way of making it sound original.

I don't remember any guilt. Nor was I disappointed. The books were all wrong: heavy petting – a rather coy expression but one I find preferable to the strictly accurate term – had taught us painlessly about our bodies, had made the act of love easier, had made the loss of her virginity less painful.

When we were dressed she made a pot of tea and we sat looking at the television like, as she put it, an old married couple. I believe that that was a turning point. I could almost wish that I had asked her to marry me then; I'd just passed my nineteenth birthday and two years wouldn't have been too long to wait, or twenty-one according to Engelsea standards too young to marry. Nor was she too old to change, too firmly rooted in Engelsea. Her accent, grotesque as it was, proved that she had aspirations to live in a different world from the one she was brought up in; but it would have made me a rather better human being, perhaps even a better writer, to have awakened with that face beside me during my youth.

I might have understood more about women, I might have understood more about marriage, I might have understood more about love. I might have hurt fewer people, used fewer people; I have not been as promiscuous as most men in my position would have been, I've liked and respected most of the women I've been to bed with, but I can't escape the fact that I've never considered anyone's feelings but my own. I've had my passions, I've known what the *coup de foudre* really means, but the thunder was soon over. I've never done anything foolish on account of a woman, I've never, when it came to it, committed myself. I've looked upon other people as specimens all my life; it's only now, looking back at what really happened for the first time, that I can perceive it. In my work I perceive it despite myself, though I've covered my tracks so well that no-one else has perceived it. Some, particularly those behind the Iron Curtain, have seen my first novel as an exposure of bourgeois morality, of the corruption of a capitalist society; but that was never further from my mind. My hero *used* the rich man's daughter, as I *used* Cora, as I've *used* every other human being I've ever known, except perhaps Maurice and Amelia.

Once when I went to the London Zoo with Maurice and Maureen and their children I saw a male and female and baby monkey huddled together big-eyed and shivering. It was rather a cold day for May, and no doubt they huddled together simply for warmth. I'm inclined to coddle myself and had read the weather forecast and was protected against the weather by a sheepskin coat and fur-lined boots and a Norwegian oiled sweater and corduroys. It strikes me now as being a fair enough summing-up of my relationship to other people: warmly wrapped up outside the bars, on the outside looking in.

This is a long way from that night in Engelsea by the roaring fire drinking strong tea, exultant at being at last a man, at having proved myself. For that was the conclusion of the sonnet; I had passed the initiation test, I had joined the club, I knew at last what it was all about. I remember unlocking the door of the staircase; though we always checked whether Lester and Amelia were asleep, one couldn't be too careful. And I remember going into the bathroom, looking down at myself with an amused pride. There was a mirror in the door of the white bathroom cabinet; I looked at my flushed face and wondered if people would be able to tell what had happened to me.

It was a very neat and clean little bathroom considering that there were two young children in the house; there were always clean towels on the heated towel-rail, and the white-painted airing cupboard was always full of neatly stacked towels and linen. The walls were lime-green with a pattern of fishes; the olive green tiles on the lower half and the floor had been laid by my father, and Hetty had made the matching lime-green towelling curtains and WC cover and bathmat and the surround at the base of the WC. I remember washing my face and hands with Palmolive and taking great pleasure in its scent which at that moment seemed almost voluptuous. And I remember thinking of Cora's breasts and the dark mystery between her thighs, now a mystery no longer, and I remember her contorted face before the act itself.

Yes, I remember. And I remember my father and Hetty coming home, not drunk but cheerful, bringing in the smell of beer and tobacco and cockles and mussels and the cold night air. And I remember walking Cora home and kissing her goodnight on the doorstep. Yes, I remember, I remember all this and more besides. I walked home along the Front and a wind had sprung up and now and again drove salt spray in my face. I'm good at remembering, it has made me a Name and brings me in £30,000 a year. But I do not remember feeling any love for her, only gratitude – my compliments to the chef, waiter, for a superb dinner – and I do not remember mentioning marriage. Nor did I ever once try to put myself in her shoes. The worst of it is that I don't think I've changed much since then.

Twelve

During the month after that, we went to the cinema twice, and to a dance at the Co-op Hall; somehow or other the opportunity to do anything more than snatch a kiss never presented itself. We didn't do any more baby-sitting. I can't pretend that I spent the whole month in a state of frustrated lust: I was now a man, I knew what it was all about and, more frequently than ever before, my body gave me involuntary relief.

But the woman to whom I clung shuddering in my dreams wasn't Cora but Jane Badingham. It was like the story of the farmer who was asked which he preferred out of all the numerous sexual activities he indulged in, and who said wet dreams, because you met a better class of person. What Miranda had said about her liking me had stuck in my mind; but I didn't see what was to be done about it until one night in late spring at the Coble.

It was raining hard and I was feeling extraordinarily elated. For me there's always excitement in the sound of the rain against the windows as much as in the feel of it against my face; even when my life has been at its most humdrum level it has always seemed to me to promise something was going to happen, that change was on its way.

Miranda was already there when I arrived, talking to Ted Lewis, who appeared a little put out. I noticed for the first time how full his mouth was and that when he pushed his hair out of his eyes he did so with a curiously coquettish flick of the wrist. 'He did ask me to have a word with you,' Miranda was saying in a low voice.

'Yes,' said Ted. 'My face doesn't fit. No need to explain.'

'No, no, darling. We all like you – ' She broke off. I kissed her on the cheek. Ted subsided in his seat, staring at his pint. I thought his eyes were wet, but didn't want to embarrass him; not for the first or last time I wanted to be invisible. No other members of the Gang were there; I was earlier than usual.

'Hello, darling,' Miranda said to me. 'You look very pink and healthy.'

'I came along by the Front.'

'You're early.'

I glanced at Ted. 'I'll leave you if you like.' She smiled. 'You're getting very perceptive. Isn't he, Ted?'

'Too bloody perceptive,' Ted said. His face was indeed the same type as Ralph's but his skin was smooth and now that I examined it olive rather than sallow. The shape was an oval, strangely Elizabethan, and Ralph's inclined towards the rectangular, it was beginning to be tired.

'We were just discussing what Ted's going to do,' Miranda said.

'Now he's got his degree,' Ted said in a high voice. 'His lousy Pass degree. She talks to you at her house, Tom, but for me it's the Coble . . .' His eyes definitely were filling with tears.

'I'm going to wash my hands,' I said and went to the Gents'. It was a large Gents' with ten compartments, the brasswork and chrome were newly polished and it smelled of carbolic. There was a washbasin and roller towel and a mirror; after I'd used the urinal I actually did wash my hands; the towel was newly laundered, and that was a small but definite pleasure to begin a promising evening. I combed my hair at the mirror; it was nearly due to be cut and there was the beginning of a wave in it; looking over my shoulder I indented the wave. I smiled at my reflection in the mirror: a pleasant open face with regular features and good teeth. No pimples, pink-and-white skin, almost a pretty boy. I scowled at my reflection and lit a cigarette: I did look a little like Jimmy Cagney but not at all tough and not at all like a writer. I shrugged my shoulders in a gesture learned from Charles Boyer and walked slowly back to the Bar Parlour.

Ted's eyes had dried and he seemed cheerful, almost too much so.

'Thought you'd fallen in,' he said. He drained his pint. 'Come on, let's get some ale in.'

I sat down beside him and rang the bell. Miranda handed me some silver. 'Get me a large Scotch, ducky. I'm without transport, the old jalopy's in dry dock. And Max has taken his to Sheffield – sounds as if he were giving it a day out, doesn't it? So I may as well get the teeniest bit sloshed.'

I had never seen her look better; she had a scarlet dress, a gold bangle and necklet and sheer stockings through which I could see the fine dark hairs. Her eyes were very bright and her face was flushed but not with rouge. Ted looked somehow depleted: it was too neat and hackneyed an image, but I couldn't help thinking of the legend of the vampire. He looked tired, as if some energy had drained away; she didn't have that effect upon me, but perhaps I was the same kind of person.

Jane Badingham came in with Bill and Nina Abercorn and instantly I forgot about everyone else. When last I'd seen her – at 3am in a brass-railed double bed in the shelter at Victoria Park, to be specific – she'd been naked, with her hair a dark cloud down to her waist. To see her again and to know that she wouldn't disappear when I opened my eyes was an enormous pleasure, secret and wild yet solid and measurable. She had a dark green button-through dress which didn't really suit her, which almost succeeded in making her look drab and swarthy. But it was merely the camera part of me which saw this; the human being called Tom Metfield saw a woman whom he wanted and who, as he caught her eye, was certain for a split second wanted him.

I rose and kissed Nina and Jane; this was a Gang ritual, and at that time and place very daring. It has now even reached the working-classes who then kissed socially only their wives or husbands or relations or small children. Then, particularly to a boy of nineteen, it was enormously titillating.

I sat down beside Jane. 'Where's Harvey?'

'Gone to a conference in bloody Edinburgh.'

'What a shame.'

She smiled. 'Your hair's growing wavy.'

'It needs cutting.'

'Don't. It looks nicer like that. You're not a bloody convict, are you?'

'I like your dress,' I said.

'I don't. It looked all right when I put it on, but now I'm sure I should never have bought the bloody thing. But darling Mummy was against it so of course I had to be contrary. Do you ever do things like that?'

'My mother's dead.'

She put her hand on mine. 'I'm sorry, love. Funny, I never knew that about you. Harvey talks about politics all the time, and you talk about books.'

'Does that bore you?'

'You've got to do something about the world, haven't you? Else there'll be no world. And I like books. But I'm very stupid really.' Her dress buttoned up to the neck; she unfastened the two top buttons. Her skin was very creamy.

'You have a degree.'

'Got it for good attendance. I met Harvey in my third year and it put me off rather . . . Do you miss your mother?'

'It was a long time ago.'

'I'd miss mine. Can't get on with her and can't get on without her. She's a rampant Tory – Harvey and she have some real old up-and-downers. She enjoys it really. Daddy gets on fine with Harvey, oddly enough. They gas for hours about the war. Old Harvey killed a hell of a lot of Germans. Says he's sorry about it now, but I doubt it myself . . . Have you any brothers or sisters?'

'A stepbrother and a half-sister. The stepbrother's a little sod, but the little girl is nice.'

'I saw you with her once when I was out with Harvey in the car. She was holding your hand and looking up at you as if you were God Almighty. I thought you were rather a prick till then.' She stopped. 'God, my language! It's Harvey's fault really. Still thinks he's in the Army.' She looked in the direction of Ted, who was now talking about Christopher Fry with Bill and Nina. 'Ralph isn't here. I don't think he will be. Do you ever have the feeling of things being arranged?'

'Sometimes,' I said. 'It's worked out well for me.'

'Your own way might have been better . . . Funny me not knowing your mother was dead. Do you get on with your stepmother?'

I shrugged. 'She's quite decent. She gets on with my father, and that's the main thing.'

'Love,' she said. 'Apropos of nothing at all, what about love?'

It took me by surprise. I know now that she intended that it should, that she deliberately was building up sexual tension. But I hadn't learned the rules of the game then, and momentarily I was embarrassed. 'I don't know much about it.'

She seemed very amused by this. 'You're a card, aren't you, Tom? But you're not going to describe town halls and dance halls and fairs and pubs and markets all your life are you?'

'I'm going to be a novelist.'

'You'll have to learn about love. All by yourself . . . Or rather, with help.' She looked at Ted again. 'Something's going on. I'm not a writer, I'm just nosy . . . But sod him. Tell me about your little sister.'

'You were asking me about love.'

'That's one kind of love. Do you tell her stories?'

I nodded. I would have been more forthcoming if she'd asked me about anything else but Amelia, even about Cora. But to tell her what I felt about Amelia would, I thought, make me seem less masculine. I was wrong, of course.

'Don't be shy,' she said. 'I don't want you to be shy.' She put her hand on my knee. It was very warm.

Without interrupting the flow of her conversation with Bill and Nina and Ted, Miranda looked at both of us and smiled; it was a very quick, cold smile, a smile of self-satisfaction, the kind of smile I've seen since then on the faces of administrators when their plans are working out. Jane gave an equally quick, cold smile in return, one manipulator acknowledging another.

'I'm not shy,' I said, finding it difficult to speak the words. 'I just can't tell you all that I'm thinking.'

She took her hand from my knee. I still felt it there. 'I'd like that. If you really told me all that you were thinking. Would you if I asked you?' She put a hand to her shoulder to adjust a strap under her dress; when she'd adjusted it she let her hand fall slowly down over her breast as if both caressing and preening herself.

'There's nothing I wouldn't do if you asked me.'

'I wouldn't want any dragons killed. And you can leave all the wicked knights to prance away on their big black chargers . . . Just tell me about yourself. And then I'll tell you about myself.'

I never did, because then Roy Badgeworth and Kim Cressage and Cyril Abbott came in, full of a project for an Engelsea Little Theatre and somehow we were all drawn into the discussion. But Jane was with me, we had made contact, the dream had become as real as the sound of rain and gurgling gutters outside. When at last I found myself sitting beside her in Harvey's Morris Eight, with Miranda in the back, I was not surprised; I knew that the consequence of the arrangement would be that Jane and I would be alone together and that the purpose of having Miranda there was so that it would appear to the others that I was to be dropped first.

Though I don't want to die now, one of the reasons why I shan't complain if I do is because I've had so much, there has been so much to praise and to be thankful for. And now I praise and am thankful for the rain that night, the new moon, the sharp penetrating bark of Hemingway from inside the dark bulk of the Grange, the smell of wet grass, the smell of Jane and Miranda, the sound of the Morris's engine which Jane kept running. I put something of this into my first novel where I describe the hero's feelings when he becomes the lover of the older woman. What excited him and what excited me was the sensation

164

of crossing the frontier into forbidden territory, of making love to a woman who not only belonged to someone else but who simply by reason of her class seemed inviolate.

My hero of course was older and more experienced than I was; he had not embraced the older woman in dreams as I had embraced Jane, he was not quite so bemused with delight, lifted to so high a point. He didn't have the feeling that the whole thing was planned for him by a third party, either. But this didn't matter at the time, only afterwards, when Miranda's smile, broad and mirthless, a voyeur's grin, as she waved goodbye to us, kept returning to irritate me. All that mattered was being alone with Jane, her hand warm on my knee, very lightly moving up my thigh. The odd thing was that it didn't seem necessary for me to put my hand on her thigh; it wasn't that I didn't want to, but because it wasn't the time for that movement in the dance.

We parked on the grass verge of a lane off the Filey Road. It was still raining, and I could see the lights of Engelsea in the distance. We did not speak from the time that we left the Grange; she kept her eyes on the road, her face unsmiling, almost severe. When she stopped the car she smiled at me. She had very good teeth. 'There's a lot of questions I never asked you,' she said.

I put my hand on her thigh, feeling the shape of the suspender button and the smoothness of nylon under the wool. She drew in her breath sharply. 'We know each other well enough now.'

Suddenly she kissed me. 'It's better in the back seat. I wouldn't want you to have a nasty accident with the gear lever.' She smelled very clean but faintly of sweat, the wonderful smell of women's sweat which is so different from men's.

'Quiet for a moment,' she said when we were in the

back seat. 'Just hold me. Ah, I knew you would.' My eyes were accustomed to the darkness by now. She was faintly smiling as my hands fumbled away, touched the tufts of hair in her armpits. 'No. I don't shave them. Harvey doesn't like it.' Then she said something which for a second damped my desire. Her words were almost Cora's words. 'Be my baby. Be my greedy little baby . . .'

But the next moment as my hand went downwards and began to caress her, she abruptly lifted herself from the seat, I heard something rustle, and she bit my ear. 'Fuck me,' she whispered. 'Fuck me.' As I lunged and then all too quickly pulled away, her fingernails dug into my buttocks, 'No, stay in. *Stay in.*'

It's all in my first novel, particularly the moment of contentment which came afterwards, as we leaned back with our arms round each other. The place was different, the essential circumstances the same. Like my hero, I learned the only truth worth learning about sex: that what matters isn't the duration of the act or whether the woman has an orgasm or not but whether, quite simply, it makes the two of you happy.

What wasn't in my novel was her reply when I said that we must do this again.

'Absolutely not, darling. It was nice. Quick but nice. But I'm marrying Harvey, and I don't want any complications.'

'There needn't be any complications.'

'You must be joking.' She stroked my hair. 'I wish you wouldn't put greasy stuff on it, then it'd be nice and crisp . . . Darling, if you have it off with someone else's fiancée, you can't avoid complications . . .'

'They make life interesting,' I said.

'They make life bloody uncomfortable. No, darling,

you're my last fling. My bachelor night. I bet old Harvey has one. If he's not having one now, the bastard.' She kissed me. 'The last time on the lips. But we'll look at each other now and again and we'll remember, won't we?'

'I never forget anything.'

'No. You might wish you could one day.' She bent down and put on the garment she'd taken off. 'You like watching that, don't you?' She pulled down her slip and fastened up her dress, then leaned over to me. 'Yes, you're decent . . . I'd better take you home.'

She was silent as we drove back towards Engelsea but when we stopped at the end of Orkney Terrace she gripped my arm so fiercely that it hurt and said: 'Don't tell Miranda.' But as I walked down the street – it had gas lamps then, and I remember their warm golden light and their sibilant mutter over the sound of the rain – I brought out of storage all the evidence, remembering especially that voyeur's grin as she'd waved goodbye to us at the Grange, and I knew that Miranda had been, so as to speak, with us all the evening and that she was with me now.

Thirteen

If I'd had any sense at all I'd have told my father the whole story. He would have perceived at once that here were all the ingredients of disaster, and instantly have bundled me into the London train. He would have known that the relationship with Cora wasn't going to stay where it was; he also would have known that, whatever she said, there was no guarantee that Jane wouldn't have another last fling with me, no guarantee that she'd keep her mouth shut about it, and no guarantee that Harvey wouldn't find out in any case.

Harvey, like all the members of Miranda's Gang, made a great parade of being broadminded; but broadmindedness is an intellectual attitude and sexual jealousy a deeply-rooted instinct. And he was a trained killer.

I wasn't so stupid that I wasn't aware of all this; on the night that Jane had her last fling with me there was, mixed with my natural exultation, a sensation of danger. I felt it very strongly on my next visit to the Coble the following week.

I wonder now if he'd guessed anything. It was like a scene from a film. Miranda and I were talking about Dylan Thomas as everyone at that time did. 'A horrible little man,' she was saying. 'He was sick on my carpet once when I had my flat in Chelsea . . .' Jane was sitting opposite me; Bill Abercorn was outlining the plot of his play to her. Harvey was on my far right, arguing with Ralph Thoralby about the necessity of the writer being committed. Engagé was the term which he used. I don't think that the lights were on: the sun was just setting and for a second the amber bitter in front of me had a faintly pink tinge.

Through my head was running the line *And the wild boys innocent as strawberries* . . . when Jane looked away from Bill and smiled at me. Harvey must have caught sight of the smile out of the corner of his eye. It was over in a second, but in the film I freeze it in three shots: Jane's smile, my responding smile, Harvey's face suddenly a killer's, the eyes narrowed, the mouth set, the body an instrument of death. We unfreeze, Jane is looking at Bill, Harvey is looking at Ralph, I am looking at Miranda. And here the film stops. I am sure that Miranda had observed the interchange and had enjoyed it; but I can't say why I'm sure.

But that moment is something to praise too. For when there is danger, one is especially alive. I've never gone out of my way to meet danger nor have I ever inhabited the world of action. But if Jane that evening had been indiscreet I wouldn't have tried to stop her, I wouldn't have taken any kind of evasive measures. And I felt as I do now when I let my car pull out on the fast lane of the M1, keeping my foot down as I move up on the car in front, knowing I ought to slow down, gambling on the driver letting me past.

I knew that evening that I ought to keep away from the Coble, just as I ought to keep away from Cora. But if you can't be foolish at nineteen, when can you be foolish?

I didn't keep away from the Coble, but I never saw Harvey and Jane there again. Each time I went there, I hoped that they'd come, and would go home half-relieved and half-disappointed.

I suppose that this is why I didn't allow the affair with Cora to die a natural death. I felt that I'd been tried and found wanting by Jane; the notion of being a one-night stand for her wasn't good for my pride.

I'm certain now that she meant what she had said: I wasn't certain then, since I was incapable of seeing her as an individual at all. She was a sex object, as Cora was; she existed to gratify my desires. I had enough sense of self-preservation not to seek her out; I expected her to be drawn irresistibly back to the Coble. The fact was that I didn't want to risk being rejected by her; instead I dreamed of her writing or 'phoning, to start a stormy secret affair which would end when I decided it must end. *I can't help it,* she would sob in my arms, *I can't help it. You're wrong for me, but I can't keep away from you. I hate you. I know you're a cold, selfish bastard, I know you only want my body, I tell myself I'm throwing every-thing away for someone who doesn't give a damn for me, but it's no use* . . . And I would take her savagely, leaving her moaning, spreadeagled and shameless, and afterwards she'd kiss my hand, weeping bitterly.

I remember this fantasy as clearly as I remember what actually happened. At that period in my life Walter Mitty was in control more often than not, particularly Mitty the Great Lover. He visits me very rarely since the success of my first novel; I have learned now that I can have anything I want providing I want it strongly enough.

The effect of that particular fantasy and the memory of Jane in Harvey's Morris Eight and the certain knowledge that what had happened between me and her was now happening between Harvey and her but happening with a far greater expertise, with a practised sensuality that I'd never achieved, was that on a May evening in Victoria Park, lying in the long grass at the top of the hill near the shelter, a circle of oaks around us, I entered Cora and, despite her entreaties, was not careful.

We lay there not moving for a long time afterwards. I'm not one for the country or making love outdoors; but never before and never since have I felt so much at one with the earth and with my body, so much part of the generality of mankind. And for an instant death didn't matter, an unacknowledged burden had been lifted. *I* was *we,* and we were going to go on. And this wasn't a conscious thought but as real and assured as the sound of marching feet; and then as she spoke we were separate people, death and the passage of the hours had returned.

'It didn't hurt this time,' she said.

'It keeps on getting better.'

'You won't run away?'

'I'll look after you.' But how I'd do that, I didn't know, and regret was already beginning.

'You're heavy,' she said. I rolled away from her and watched her button up her blouse and her stockings. She reached down beside her for her knickers, drew them on quickly, then burst into tears. I tried to take her into my arms, but she pushed me away, lying on the grass with her back towards me and her thin shoulders shaking.

It was growing dark now; she sat up, hugging her knees, and stared at the purple and scarlet sunset, not speaking. I felt myself immeasurably younger than her, bewildered and rather frightened at the strength of adult emotion. It was a curiously humiliating feeling; I was absolutely cut off from her.

She began to powder her face. The smell of the grass and her powder put in my mind's eye a sudden vivid picture of a small room with a fire burning brightly in the grate, a new carpet, two new wing armchairs, and a matching sofa. On the hearthrug was an open work-box with reels of cotton and skeins of wool and a pair of dressmaker's scissors. I had a sense of desolation as the picture vanished, a vast regret and the knowledge of a long journey ahead. I gave her a cigarette and we smoked in silence. Miranda's words had had their effect: I was on my tod, I was alone, I was on the outside looking in. But at least I never thought of what had happened as a quick roll in the hay, a blow-through, getting laid; I was grateful, and I still am.

After that I did what I should have done in the first instance and used a condom. It was never quite the same again, though I won't pretend that I didn't enjoy it or that I felt any sense of guilt. I didn't mention marriage, nor did Cora; at the moment of orgasm she would sometimes gasp out an endearment, but afterwards would not reply to the endearments which I felt myself somehow forced to utter. She was now in charge of the affair; it culminated in her forbidding me to go to the Coble.

'I don't like that woman,' she said.

'She's my friend – '

'If you go with her, you can't go with me.'

'Don't be ridiculous – '

But she'd already got up and walked out of the Cochrane; I followed her out into the street and took her arm.

'I'm going home,' she said. 'I don't want to see you again.'

Then she burst out crying and I took her into an alley-way and comforted her, her tears wet on my cheek, and promised that I wouldn't see Miranda again.

This was all used in my first novel, though the younger woman's jealousy for the older one had rather a different origin and, in sharp contradiction to me, my hero wanted to marry the younger woman. What I didn't put in the novel was the scene where the younger woman tells the hero she is pregnant. My reason for this was technical: to have the pregnancy revealed by the girl's father advanced the story, gave it an extra twist. That's what I've told myself all these years. In another sense it isn't. I found a way of evading the scene in the novel because I didn't want to remember what actually was said between Cora and myself that July evening in Victoria Park.

I was hot and sweaty and irritable and – this sticks in my memory more than anything else – I'd got some black paint under my fingernails and couldn't get it out. I have an obsession about keeping my nails clean – I acquired it from Miranda – and it seemed that evening as if they'd be permanently black-rimmed. Cora did nothing to lift my spirits; she looked pasty rather than interestingly pale, and she was wearing a drab brown cotton dress which did nothing for her.

'I wanted to do some work tonight,' I said after we'd sat in silence for a while.

'Work?'

'Writing. It *is* work.'

'Damn your writing! Don't you know what I want to see you for?'

'Not if you won't tell me.'

'I've been to the doctor's.'

'What about it?'

I can't believe now that I was so obtuse, much less so

uncouth; perhaps it would have been different if she'd looked more attractive, less pasty and woebegone.

She started to cry. 'Can't you guess? Do I have to tell you?'

'Oh Christ,' I said. 'That's fucked things up, it really has.'

'There's no need for that sort of language,' she said, suddenly prim.

'*Language*,' I said, mimicking her, '*thet* sort of *lenguage* – what the hell do you expect?'

I think that I've never been crueller to anyone. I'm not the sort to feel guilty for very long, but I still feel guilty about indulging myself in gratuitous ridicule of her pathetic little pretensions at that moment. I think that if there was any love between us, I killed it then.

She perceptibly winced, then looked away from me and dried her eyes. 'What are you going to do about it then?'

'I can't understand it. We were careful – '

'You shut the stable door after the horse had bolted.' Her accent had gone and her voice was very steady.

I remembered a casual remark Miranda had once made about the consequences of a love affair and a chum in Harley Street. 'It's not too late to do something.'

'You mean get rid of it?'

'It isn't anything, not if it's done properly.'

'It won't be you it's done to, will it?'

'I could marry you.'

She shook her head. 'You don't like the way I speak, do you? What would Miranda think?' She got up. 'You arrange something then. Soon. Because if my father finds out he'll kill you, he really will.'

'I'll take you for a drink,' I said.

'No. I don't care if I don't see you again.' She turned. 'Stay where you are. I can find my own way home.'

I watched her till she was out of sight. I am forced to be honest: I felt nothing but relief as I watched her go.

I phoned Miranda from a public call-box outside the park. 'I've got to see you, Miranda.'

Her voice was cold. 'I was wondering how I'd offended you.'

'I was – busy. I can't explain – '

'You've not been busy writing, have you?'

'Oh God, Miranda, don't go on at me! I'm in a mess – '

'Come over then.'

'Now?'

'Of course now, you bloody fool.' She hung up.

Fourteen

I knew when I pressed the doorbell at the Grange that events were beginning to move despite myself; I wasn't sure that I liked the feeling. When no sound came from the doorbell I started to turn away; and if I had done, if I'd gone away to make my own arrangements to tidy up the mess I was in, then I should have broken a link in the conveyor belt, have got off it to make my own future. It might have been better, it might have been worse, but I would have decided it. But, seeing that the door was ajar, I went in. Hemingway padded towards me with his curious rolling gait, sniffed at me, and licked my hand. I patted him; he was somehow a great comfort.

Miranda, lying on the sofa in the study in a pink quilted dressing-gown, smiled as I came in.

'Don't tell me, let me guess,' she said. 'Cora's pregnant.'

I nodded and sat down. There was a thick manuscript on the floor beside her, professionally bound with a stiff back in old gold.

'Jack's novel,' Miranda said. 'Piss-poor. Christ, what shall I say to him?'

'You'll think of something,' I said.

'We've got to think of something for you now,' she said. She waved towards the drink table. 'Help yourself.'

I poured myself a whisky. 'I don't know what to do.'

'Not marry her for a start. I told you, that'd be death for you, absolute death. I don't think you'll ever be anything else but a lousy husband, anyway.'

'Thanks for the kind words.' What Cora had said to me still rankled; perhaps it was no different from what I thought myself, but it wasn't agreeable from someone else.

'Oh honey, you've got to face facts about yourself. You're just like me, you're too wrapped up in yourself, there's a part of you will never grow up. Didn't Jane spot it?'

'What's she got to do with it?'

'Nothing at all. But she's the sort of person who would be good for you. Rather too good for Harvey, who's a shit of the first water, to mix metaphors slightly.' She leaned over and patted my hand. 'Oh, love, I've been through this myself. In a different way.'

'Yes. But I've got to do something about Cora.'

'Does she want to marry you?'

'No.'

'Don't sound so resentful about it. She's got more sense than I'd thought. And she doesn't want the baby?'

'She made that clear. In a roundabout way.'

'Sensible girl.' She held out her glass. 'Get me a drink, will you?'

Suddenly I found myself shaking. I poured out her drink, emptied my own glass, and poured myself another. 'Do you know someone?' I asked. 'Someone good?'

'Very good. A chum of mine from my London days. Very good and very greedy.'

'I've got some money.'

'Not enough for him. Is it very early on?'

'She's just found out.'

'No problem then.'

'How much would he want?'

'About £100.'

'Oh Christ!'

'I'll take care of that.'

'I'll pay you back.'

'Don't worry.' She got up and took a sheet of die-stamped writing-paper from the desk and scribbled something on it. Then she tore off her own address. She gave the paper to me. 'The sooner she gets in touch with him the better.'

'Should I do that for her?'

'Leave it to me.' She looked at me with an expression of wry affection which I'd not seen before. 'Christ, you are a fool! You can't see further than your prick end, can you?'

I was still trembling. 'I'm sorry, Miranda.'

'So you ought to be. I did warn you.'

'Is it dangerous?'

'An abortion? It's no picnic, dear. But my chum's very good and very cautious. He won't do it if there's any risk. She'd better have someone sensible along with her. Not you, love, don't look so frightened. She won't want you. I don't think she'll want to see you again.'

She put down her whisky and rubbed her hands together briskly. She had long thin hands with long red nails; I had never looked at them closely before, but now I did and I found something frightening about them.

'We'd better make some new plans for your future,' she said.

'I don't feel like it. I'm going to tell her to go ahead and have the baby and I'll marry her.'

The moment I said this I began to feel better and stopped trembling.

'Don't be such a bloody fool! Look, one day you'll be

able to afford to be decent and kind and compassionate. Not that you will be – you'll always be a cold little sod. But now, my dear, you've got to consider your future.' She grinned. 'I tell you what. I'll allow you a little self-indulgence. Write a story about a young man just like you, who does the decent thing. And who buggers his whole life up and buggers the girl's life up into the bargain.'

What I said in reply is irrelevant to my story – which is her story. I knew that she was right and, whatever it makes me, I couldn't stand out against her. I didn't write the story which she suggested, of course. Stories – for me at least – aren't written in that way. But I wrote it later in my first novel when the hero disgustedly rejects the rich man's suggestion of an abortion for his daughter. I'm not so much cold as economical: I waste nothing, and can recognize good advice when I'm given it.

Fifteen

Jessie Ramelton was Cora's first cousin, dark-haired like
Cora, but skinny rather than slim, and with a large nose
which would have looked better on a man. As I went
towards the café on the other side of the square from the
Coble, she barred my entrance.

'Cora won't be there,' she said. Her eyes were very
bright and her sallow cheeks flushed.

'Did she tell you?'

'She's not coming.'

'She could have 'phoned.'

'She's ill. Much you care.'

'It isn't any business of yours.' It was a sparkling
evening with a cool breeze from the sea; there were several
old men standing around the square, smoking their pipes
and looking at the sea with, or so I imagined, the respect-
ful friendliness one has for an old enemy when the war
is long over; by the café was a group of youths and teenage
girls giggling at whatever makes girls giggle at that age.
So we had a potential audience; I turned away.

She caught my arm. 'I took her to Scarborough, you pig.'

I shook my arm free; already two girls were looking at
us. 'I'll go and see her.'

'She doesn't want to see you.'

'She can tell me herself.'

'You still haven't asked how she is.'

'All right, how is she?'

'Oh, she's not going to *die* or anything. But she feels awful. *You* wouldn't understand. You're so clever, and you wouldn't understand.'

'I'll see her when she's better.' I walked away towards the Coble. She ran after me and caught hold of my arm and spat in my face. 'Pig,' she said, 'Dirty selfish pig. You watch out, you pig.'

There was silence; then everyone seemed to be looking at me and a hum of excited conversation broke out. I wiped my cheek and half-ran into the Coble. It wasn't a moment I should care to relive. But relive it I did; it was the nucleus of an incident in my first novel and in my fourth novel too. When I calculate it by money earned per hundred words my humiliation was salved by some £2,000. But when I think about it now the humiliation returns: that ugly, spiteful, stupid girl spoke the plain truth.

When I bolted inside the Coble I went straight to the Gents' and washed my face; it was early in the evening and the roller-towel was freshly clean. There was even a new cake of Lifebuoy soap in the washbasin. There was only Ted Lewis in the Lounge Bar when I went in; he was lighting a cigarette and in the ashtray in front of him one still smouldered.

'Hi,' I said. 'No-one here yet?'

'Of course there's no-one here yet,' he said petulantly. 'Why do people say bloody silly things like that?'

I pressed the bell. A waiter came in whom I hadn't seen before, a small square man with a cropped grey head.

'Where's Cyril?' I asked Ted when the barman had left.

'Up to here in it.' Ted waved at his neck.

'What's he done?'

'Well, you've *seen* him. What do you think he's done?'

'OK, OK.' I didn't like Ted's attitude, but I wanted no more scenes that evening.

'I'm going into the bloody Army. Education Corps.' He delivered the information like an insult.

'Miranda's good advice?'

'Oh, fuck her. My own idea actually. So everyone's against it. Do you ever get fed up with good advice?'

I nodded.

'But you know what you want to do, don't you?'

'Up to a point.'

'But you can do something. I can't do anything – '

There were footsteps at the entrance and his face changed to a smile, then relapsed as Jack Barrington came in, carrying under his arm a black rexine music case with something bulky inside it.

He sat down opposite me, grunting briefly at us both. These grunts served him as greeting; it was as if actually to speak a greeting would cost him money. He stared at us for a minute, his pale blue eyes unwinking, then leaned over the table to Ted.

'Would you be aware now of whether Ralph would be honouring us with his presence?'

'He was very vague,' Ted said. The question seemed to irritate him. 'Some committee meeting or other.'

'Umph.' Jack took out his pipe. He began to clean it with an attachment from a large bone-handled penknife. He saw me looking at the penknife. 'Got that when I was a wee laddie,' he said. 'Used every one of these feddadles except the one for taking stones out of horses' hooves.'

'Very nice,' I said.

'I wanted to ask Ralph a favour, you see.'

I guessed what the favour was. Miranda had put her thumbs down on his novel, and he wanted a fresh verdict from Ralph. The suspicion was confirmed later in the evening when, Miranda's name having been mentioned, he said:

'She's clever enough, but she's out of touch. Ten years ago she may have been on the ball, but now the world has passed her by.' He looked at me meaningly. 'Now, you haven't her experience, her sheer know-how, but you know what goes *now* . . .'

Soon after that I made some excuse and went out; for all that I know Jack gave the manuscript to Ted. It had been the most depressing evening I'd ever had at the Coble; though Miranda's Gang could still generate its special glamour without Miranda, three was too few and we were in any case the wrong three. Precisely because I hadn't liked my company I'd drunk too much; precisely because I'd drunk too much I went to Cora's home with some hazy idea in my head of justifying myself – of proving, I suppose, that I wasn't entirely a dirty selfish pig.

I knew that I'd made a mistake when I saw Cora's father at the door. He had very broad shoulders which seemed to fill up the doorway. He said nothing, but closed the door behind him and half dragged me into the alleyway half up the street. Still silent, he hit me on the jaw; as I came back, my fists up but a second too slowly, he hit me in the eye. A part of my mind noted amongst the pain that the cliché of seeing stars was entirely accurate. But the worst pain was when I tried to dodge a blow and it landed on my left ear. He hit me again on the jaw; I went back and – another cliché being found to be entirely accurate – the ground rushed up and hit the back of my head.

I struggled to my feet with the notion of hitting him, but felt too sick to carry the notion into effect. 'I'll kill you,' I said, and retched.

He laughed, his hands at his sides. 'I'd finish you off properly, but at least you were man enough to come to our house. Just you listen, sonny. Don't come near my daughter again.'

I was violently sick; when I recovered myself, my hand on the wall for support, he looked at me in disgust for a moment. 'You're a fine bloody sight now, aren't you?' He slapped my face. 'If I were you, I'd leave Engelsea. I mean that, sonny.'

He turned; I wiped my face with my handkerchief and began to dust my clothes down. I heard footsteps and looked up to see Sergeant Harris. Cora's father was six feet and he stood a good four inches over him; he weighed seventeen stone and very little of it was fat. I'd never used him because he was altogether too good to be true, the huge tough copper who stood no nonsense but who knew when to leave well enough alone.

'Had an accident, Mr Metfield?'

'I fell.'

'Quite a fall, that. Young chap like you should be steadier on his feet.' He turned to Cora's father. 'Not quite in your class, is he, Bob? Big difference in height and weight there, Bob. Why, he's nobbut a lad.'

'You bloody know me. I had good reason.'

'So you say. How's Cora? Haven't seen her around.'

'Look, if you want to make a charge, make a charge.'

The Sergeant shook his head. 'The lad's fallen.' He sniffed. 'Can't hold his ale yet. Well, it isn't a crime, unless he makes a nuisance of himself. But I wouldn't like him to fall again.'

Cora's father grunted something which I didn't quite catch and walked away slowly. His shoulders seemed to droop.

'What it is to be a father,' the Sergeant said. 'You all right?' He ran his hands up and down my chest quickly and expertly. I nodded.

'Better get home and get cleaned up then. Just tell your father something. I'm having no vendettas in this town. Right?'

'I'll tell him.'

He smiled. 'You know what? We pay for our pleasures, don't we?'

I didn't answer him because I was frightened I'd be sick again, but his smile broadened and became a laugh. He was still laughing as I walked away.

When I got home my father and Hetty were looking at the TV. My father glanced at me, but didn't change his expression. Hetty gasped. 'You're hurt – '

'Get cleaned up,' my father said. He put his glasses away and switched off the TV. 'Make some tea, Hetty.'

I was almost afraid to look at myself in the bathroom mirror, but once I'd washed myself and straightened my tie and brushed my clothes I didn't look as badly damaged as I felt. But the bruise over my eye was already taking on a purple tinge and my left ear was reddened and swollen and aching. There didn't seem to be anything broken, and I still had all my teeth. I brushed them and gargled with Listerine and took two Alka-Seltzers; now the taste of vomit had been washed from my mouth and my stomach began to settle down.

When I came down into the living-room my father and Hetty were drinking tea.

'You poor boy,' Hetty said, and came towards me.

'Poor boy be damned,' said my father. 'Take your tea upstairs, Hetty. I'll have a quiet word with him.'

'But what happened?'

'I'll tell you in the morning.'

She shrugged and went out of the room. She wasn't generally so meek and biddable; it was merely that over the years she and my father had agreed on the boundaries of their authority over their children. And of course I wasn't her son.

My father poured me a cup of tea. 'How's the other chap?'

'*He's* all right.'

'Who was it?'

'Cora's father.'

'The bastard! Christ, he could eat you for breakfast.' He stood up. 'We'll see about that bugger. I'll teach him to pick on someone his own size.'

Somehow as he stood up he'd turned into a killing machine, his fists were clenched, his eyes narrowed, his body set in a boxer's crouch; I remembered him telling me once that there were things he'd learned in the Army that he'd never forgotten.

'Sergeant Harris has a message for you. He doesn't want any vendettas.'

My father pulled a face and sat down. 'And what the hell was he doing to let it happen?'

'He didn't come along till after.'

'That's a lot of bloody use. All right, you tell me why you were clobbered.'

'I got Cora pregnant.'

'That's no surprise. Took two of you, though. Want to marry her?'

'She got rid of it.'

'Well then, that's settled.' He was silent for a moment. 'Funny how things change.'

'She didn't want to marry me either. It was the only sensible thing to do.'

'Oh aye. If your mother and I had been sensible, you wouldn't have been here, would you?'

'Don't go on at me, Dad, I've had enough for one day.'

186

'It's done now, isn't it? I suppose you know you've broken the law?'

'There won't be any trouble.' I got up. 'I'm going to bed.'

'Sit down!' He rapped out the words. 'Who did she go to? An old woman in a back street? You may still be in trouble.'

'I told you, there won't be any trouble. It was a surgeon. He's supposed to be a good one.'

'And how would she find out about him?'

'She didn't. Look, Dad, it's all over. Let's forget it – '

'You tell me how she found out. Or I'll finish the job off that Cora's father began.'

He meant it. I had never seen him so angry.

'Miranda arranged it.'

His anger suddenly evaporated and his face seemed to grow older. 'Miranda. You're in a mess, so who do you go to? Miranda. Not your own father.'

'I'm sorry. I thought you'd be angry – '

'For Christ's sake, I've been young myself.' He seemed to recover himself. 'Women . . . We can't do with 'em and we can't do without 'em. Do you know what my old Dad used to say? The trouble with cunt, lad, is the women have all of it . . .' He poured rum into his tea and then into mine. 'Well, you've had a lucky escape. I suppose your savings have gone for a Burton, but the lesson's cheap at the price.'

'Miranda paid.'

'Miranda! And how much?' His anger had returned.

'It doesn't matter. I'll pay her back.'

'How much?'

'A hundred,' I muttered.

He took out his cheque book and scribbled out a

cheque. He stood up. 'Wonder she doesn't bloody well adopt you. Get up.'

'Where are we going?'

'To see Mrs Bloody Abberwick. About time she learned you'd got a father. And not to interfere with other folk's children. Because you are a child. Your prick's grown ahead of your brain.'

'We can't go now – '

He gave me a push which knocked me out of my chair. 'Come on.'

'We could 'phone – '

'Fuck that. I can't send a cheque over the 'phone.'

I argued with him all the way to the Grange. Though argue is hardly the correct word; I asked him repeatedly either to turn back or let me go in by myself, and he remained silent and scowling, driving the van at a speed which at any other time would have appalled me. But when we'd skidded to a stop outside the Grange he handed the cheque to me.

'All right. I won't make you look small. But pay her it. And tell her you've got a father.'

I found my eyes moistening. 'Thanks.' I squeezed his shoulder.

I pressed the bell but there was no sound. The door stood ajar a little. I went into the hall; there was no line of light from under the drawing-room door or the door of Max's den. The wall-lights – candle type bulbs with plastic collars round the stem to simulate candles – were on in the hall but not the big overhead chandelier. There was an oak chest in one corner, and a Victorian davenport in another. Over the fireplace was a large oil painting of a fat man in a wig and riding-coat. He had a look of Max. I was putting off the confrontation; I half-ran into Miranda's study.

The lights weren't on but there was a red glow from a small electric fire and as I opened the door light came in from the passage.

'Miranda,' I said, my eyes passing the information of a shape on the sofa to my brain, and my brain on the evidence of former visits to the room interpreting the white shape as Miranda. 'Miranda, I've got to give you this.' The cheque in my hand, I went towards the sofa; there was now a smell which, in a puzzled way, my brain interpreted as the smell of the beach at low tide and then, for what seemed like five full minutes but in fact would have been no more than five seconds, received the information that Miranda was with Ralph Thoralby on the sofa and they were both naked. Ralph's head jerked up towards me; Miranda was wearing a gold chain and cross, there was a small sickle-shaped birthmark beneath her left breast, there was a little heap of clothes at the foot of the sofa. I put the cheque on the coffee table and walked out. I think that Miranda called out my name, but my left ear had begun to throb and I felt sick again.

Outside in the fresh air the sickness passed but my ear still hurt. (I found out the next day that the perforation had been reopened.) I stared at the tennis court: the new moon had come out from behind the clouds and I could distinguish the colours of the flowers in the rock borders on the lawn behind it. I only knew that I had been betrayed, that I'd lost the most valuable possession that I had ever had, that I was dirtied irretrievably, that I had somehow lost my manhood; and all the time my memory was fitting events – trivial and disregarded at the time – into the conclusion of the two naked bodies on the sofa, and the cold part of me was noting all that I saw and smelled and heard and touched, all to be stored away for the future.

Sixteen

A huge drunken man is lurching along the pavement. His fists are clenched and he dribbles obscenities. His face – low forehead, bloodshot eyes, unshaven jowls, blackened teeth – is contorted with hate. His bloodstained shirt is torn open at the neck, the knot of his tie is behind his ear. There is a razor slash across his cheek, his muscles strain the cheap cloth of his jacket, he stinks of sweat and vomit. He doesn't look where he's going, but everyone makes way for him. No-one who looks at him feels safe until they're out of his sight. If he notices anyone, man, woman, or child, he'll knock them down and deliberately, ponderously, kick them to death. He is, as the saying goes, spoiling for a fight. He would, as the saying goes, kill you as soon as look at you.

That is my image of God. If I were to have a prayer it would be: please, God, don't single me out, please, God, leave me alone. And He has left me alone, I've had a marvellous life, I have a marvellous life now. Mine is a success story and let there be no doubt about it. And let there be no doubt about success being thoroughly enjoyable, about champagne being nicer than beer and caviare than frozen fish fingers. Ever since the publication of my first novel I've been one of our society's pampered darlings, and I've relished every moment of it.

Was it simply a question, though, of God leaving me alone? Isn't there a further development of the image? The scowl on the drunk's face is replaced by a smile, the big hard hand shakes yours, the heavy arm drops affectionately on your shoulder, you're his dear old friend, he drags you into the nearest bar, plies you with double brandies, gives you a large cigar, invites a couple of girls to the table, looks at you with brimming eyes and swears that all he has is yours, and presses a bulging wallet into your hand to prove it – men in that state can go as easily in one direction as the other. His liking has nothing to do with merit or even with you liking him.

But if it ends at this very moment, if His mood suddenly changes and I find myself, so as to speak, flat on the floor amidst broken glass, His foot descending on my face, then there have been over twenty years which were more good than bad, and four of them almost without flaw.

There are some things I have missed. I remember once when I was staying with Maurice and Maureen in their little house near Chertsey. There was a fair-sized garden at the back which my bedroom overlooked. Beyond the garden was a wood, mostly conifers. It was a fine June morning, a little cold for the time of year; I awoke early and couldn't get to sleep again. The window was open and the smell of grass and pines blew in. I was working on *Vanguard* at that time and shared a flat off Holland Road with two other journalists. The house was so new that the plaster hadn't dried out yet; with its single divan bed and cream bedside table and wardrobe and dressing-table it should have been bare and cheerless but wasn't. It was my room in the flat off Holland Road which now seemed bare and cheerless in comparison.

I went downstairs and made tea in the tiny kitchen; I had borrowed a pair of Maurice's pyjamas and had had to roll the bottoms up. I was wearing his woollen dressing-gown, which again was too big for me, but I was glad of its warmth. I took the tray upstairs and knocked at Maurice and Maureen's bedroom door. When I entered, their five-year-old daughter Sarah was lying between them. They each had an arm round her. She was a sturdy round-faced child with fair hair; she had bright yellow pyjamas on and was awake and smiling.

'She always comes in at seven,' Maureen said. 'Our little alarm clock.'

Maurice yawned. Sarah ran her fingers over his chin. 'Gosh, I've got a hangover,' he said. 'You darn bachelors . . .'

What moved me almost to tears was their unity, their vulnerability, their vast simplicity and innocence. I felt incomplete looking at them, cold and lonely and sterile. I was finishing my first novel then and it kept me in a state of more or less permanent euphoria; but as I looked at the three of them I wasn't any longer aware of what I had got but of what I hadn't got. It was shortly after that that I met Jean – with marriage in my mind but, I suspect now, the wrong kind of marriage. Whatever it was that I felt to exist between Maurice and Sarah and Maureen was never there for us.

I remember another family who sat opposite me on the Tube, a dowdy couple in their late forties, with a daughter in her twenties. It was a Friday night and each had full carrier bags. It was last summer; the husband had a cream linen jacket and grey flannels and open sandals and grey socks; his wife and daughter had print dresses and cardigans. All three wore spectacles, the mother and daughter those of the harlequin kind, which might perhaps do something for a pretty girl, but did nothing for them except to underline their extreme plainness. I could in my mind's eye see their semi-detached house – not, I thought, a Council house – in Harrow or Wembley, one of a long row of similar houses, each with its neat little front garden, each different in some way trifling to the casual observer but all-important to its owner, and absurdly and touchingly, having names rather than numbers.

They didn't speak to each other but I felt on no other evidence but my instincts that they were happy and complete, that they'd be tired from their small festival of a day's shopping in the West End, that they'd be looking forward to a drink of tea and unpacking their purchases. The wife had a carrier from C & A; I could imagine the long pleasurable rite of selection. Women appreciate the importance of money – which after all is the tangible representation of so many hours of our life – and of material things far more intensely than men. I don't suppose it likely that I'll ever see them again or that our paths will ever cross. But for days afterwards and even now they stick in my mind. What they had was what Maurice and Sarah and Maureen had and what I, because I'm the sort of person I am, have never had: they were a family, they loved each other without complication, they were safe and warm as long as God didn't decide to put the boot in. And I, like all pampered darlings, want what I haven't got expressly and especially since someone else has it, the rich man envious of the poor man's one ewe lamb.

The envy is ephemeral. I'm essentially lonely, I have few friends, it might almost be said that I live without human love. But it's what I've chosen or, rather, what Miranda helped me to choose. Looking back over the twenty years since leaving Engelsea I can see now that my life has been as if planned by her at every stage.

There were the bad moments: after I burst in upon her and Ralph I went through the worst period of depression in my whole life. It wasn't made easier to bear by the pain I had from my damaged ear, which cost me a month of sleepless nights. I can't say that I felt any guilt about Cora; my beating-up seemed to have made us even. The nearest I came to guilt was that now and again what my father had said would lodge itself unbidden in my mind: if he'd been as sensible as me I wouldn't have been born.

Mostly, though, what I had in my mind was Miranda. I wasn't in the least bothered by her being unfaithful to Max who was, as far as I was concerned, a non-person. Jealousy may have had something to do with it; I didn't want her to give any time to anyone except me. And she was of course – to use psychological jargon is unavoidable – a mother-figure profaned. At that age naturally I didn't care whether she had sexual needs, much less whether Ralph had. Perhaps I would have been hurt less if I'd thought that she was overcome by passion; but I suspected that she was administering sex therapeutically, that she was trying to straighten Ralph out; and even at nineteen I was adult enough to know that people are best left alone, no matter how untidy or sordid their lives may appear, that they're settled and cosy in their particular slum, near the shops and the pubs and the bingo parlours, always with something going on, and if you transfer them to a brand-new flat in a brand-new high-rise block at a rent they can't afford, they'll be desperately isolated, staring out of the twentieth floor over a windswept wasteland, and will probably be blown to pieces by the brand-new high-efficiency central heating system into the bargain.

I doubt if I put it together as neatly as this at the time; for on top of it all I had to cope with the usual glandular turmoils of nineteen. But these are the same for every generation. Nor do I want to remember in detail how depressed I was. I hadn't been through it before, so I couldn't visualize it coming to an end. I didn't go out very much, and not at all to the Coble; I didn't want to see anyone who knew me, least of all Miranda.

To do him justice, there were no recriminations from my father. Indeed, I think in a way he was rather proud of me, as being a chip off the old block, a bit of a lad. And Hetty looked upon the Cora affair with an amused indulgence; it was what you'd expect from a boy of nineteen.

I went to the shop with a black patch over my eye, took a great many aspirins, to keep off the pain in my ear, went to the cinema a great deal, read a great deal, began many articles and finished none. Amelia was my great consolation, though I naturally didn't tell her about Cora. The only time when I wasn't actively depressed, in fact, was when she was sitting on my knee looking at TV or I was sitting on her bed telling her a story. But even this could hurt: sometimes when I was finally dropping off to sleep at night, my ear still throbbing, I would awaken with a start, seeing the small thin body mangled under a car, a small hand emerging from a stormy sea and disappearing, hearing a thin little voice carried away by the wind.

That was when I first began to hate God and when I determined to do without love as far as I was able.

I can't set a date to this decision – it was a gut decision rather than a conscious decision. But once I'd made it the depression began to lift and the pain in my ear went away.

One evening – I think it must have been later that summer – I told my father that I wanted to leave Engelsea. He turned the TV off.

'I was watching it,' Hetty said.

'You were bloody well knitting. It's a load of crap anyway.' He pointed towards the kitchen. 'Make us some tea, love.' Hetty got up and went out without a word. This puzzled me a little at the time, but it doesn't now; she could already see Lester in my place in the shop.

'I can't stick it here any more,' I said.

'You don't have to go for me. And if Cora's father gets awkward I'll pawse the bugger senseless, big though he is.'

'I'd have gone anyway.'

'I think you would have gone away, even without that Abberwick women to make you discontented. You don't really belong here. God knows where you do belong. Pity you won't be going into the Forces . . .' He looked at me with a bleak affection. 'Won't do you any harm to stand on your own two feet . . . Not that you'll be going all that far away.'

'Not far away?' For I already had a vision of London and a new life which was somehow to be – against all logic – the facsimile of Miranda's Chelsea phase after the publication of *Moving Through*.

'I had a word with your Grandfather Knossington. Sanctimonious old bugger. He's been pulling strings. He and a few other bloody Knossingtons. You're to see the editor of the *Charbury Gazette*.'

'You might have told me.'

'You might have told me when you got Cora into trouble. Cuts both ways. You don't *have* to see the editor. Get some bloody awful job in London if you like.'

I had the same helpless feeling that I had as a child; I would ask my Grandfather Knossington for money for the cinema or circus or sweets and the large head would turn slowly towards me and consider the request in silence, the pale blue eyes frowning under the heavy dark

eyebrows, the deep creases from the nose to the corners of
the mouth deepening still further; the decision would be
declined in a monosyllable and the head would turn away
from me. And if I disagreed with his decision there was
no point in argument; he just wasn't interested.

'That's it, then,' I said.

'The Knossingtons want you out, lad.'

'I suppose I should thank him.'

'I'm afraid he doesn't want to see you, Tom.' My
father's tone was unusually gentle.

'He never liked me anyway,' I said bitterly.

'It isn't you he doesn't like. It's me. *Bad blood*, the old
sod said to me, *there's bad blood in that lad*. I know
damned well whose bad blood he means . . .' He laughed.
'Don't look so woebegone. Funny thing, if you'd been a
good lad and not put a bun in Cora's oven, he'd have done
nothing for you. But you were a bad lad and went at her
hammer-and-tongs. So the old bugger sets to thinking
what's the one thing you want, the one thing that'll shift
you out of Engelsea. I don't know what the moral of that
is.'

The one thing you want; despite my dreams of London
I was well aware, thanks to Miranda, that one didn't get
a job in Fleet Street without provincial experience. A job
in the *Gazette* would be exactly what she'd planned for
me; but she hadn't got me the job, I'd got it by having
sexual intercourse with Cora. The moral – and a subsidiary theme in my first novel and the primary theme in
my second – was that we're not rewarded according to our
merits, that the wicked – or at any rate the reckless and
sensual and selfish – shall flourish like the green bay tree.

From that evening on my life without Miranda began.
As I look through the storehouse, pulling out reel after

reel of unedited film, I congratulate myself on my thrift. There is so much I haven't used yet, more than enough for the rest of my life. There are the four years in Charbury, the six years on the staff of *Vanguard,* the two years in Fleet Street on the *Argus*; then there's my marriage in 1964, the year of the publication of my first novel, and my divorce five years afterwards. Come to that, there are my early years in Charbury and Engelsea – it's like discovering substantial back accounts one had forgotten.

I did see Miranda again after leaving Engelsea, but only once. For in the winter of 1953 Max, by some foreign exchange *legerdemain* of the kind I can never quite understand, acquired a villa in the South of France and she began to spend more and more time there. And when I visited Engelsea I spent most of my time with my father and Hetty and Amelia. Later, when I bought my house after the publication of my novel, I preferred to have them stay with me; from the time that Max died in 1965 to the morning that Deirdre walked out of my house I didn't visit Engelsea at all. There had of course been a great deal of publicity in connection with my divorce, which didn't matter at all in London, but would have been hard to put up with in Engelsea. But that wasn't entirely the reason. There was some sort of discontent in me which I could control in London but felt I wouldn't have been able to control in Engelsea.

I told Deirdre about this recently and she said, rather contemptuously: 'You're a wonderful hand at excuses.'
'Excuses for what?'
'Whatever it is that's on your conscience.'
'I've nothing on my conscience.'
'Nothing to congratulate yourself for, either.'

'I've not done so badly for a boy who left school at fifteen.'

'And you did it all by yourself.' Her voice was flat.

'Yes, all by my bloody self. Me and no-one else.'

I knew it wasn't true even as I said it. I use the phrase *my life without Miranda* without hesitation; but have I really lived without her? Hasn't my life from the time I met her run along the lines planned by her? Does it make any difference to the soldier in action that the general who planned the battle isn't actually by his side?

Yes, I had plenty of excuses for not keeping in touch with her, of course. My shock at discovering her with Ralph did me good service for some four years. I couldn't see her as Miranda any longer, but merely as a pair of big slack breasts with big tobacco-brown nipples. I didn't, or so I told myself, respect her any more, I couldn't be at my ease with her.

Then she had a drinking problem for about six years – that would be the time I left the *Gazette* to go to *Vanguard*. It was my father, oddly enough, who made me aware of her problem – reminded me, in fact, of her existence – on my second visit home from London.

I go to that part of the storehouse with reluctance, take out the dusty reel of film, set up the projector. Saturday evening, a warm June; there are new orange and yellow curtains on the living-room windows, and a new cherry-coloured fitted carpet and a new three-piece suite – pale fawn moquette, rather too big for the room. Hetty is knitting, Amelia, tall and leggy now, is reading *Anne of Green Gables*. My father is reading the paper. Lester is brushing his shoes in the kitchen.

'You don't seem to see anything of Mrs Abberwick now,' my father says.

'She's always away.'

'Doesn't stop you 'phoning her now.'

It was an order.

I edit the rest of the reel. Miranda was there in the Lounge Parlour at the Coble, and so was the Gang; but it was a new Gang. Out of the fourteen people there with Miranda I only knew Ralph Thoralby: the new members seemed younger than the Old Gang, and there were only two girls among them.

Miranda was sitting on the upholstered bench against the wall. It had been re-upholstered in a shiny black material which was a curiously accurate match of her hair in colour and texture. She was wearing more rouge than I ever remembered her using, and her white linen dress showed the division between her breasts. She had always had a certain flamboyance, but now she looked almost whorish; I liked the change no more than I liked the new Gang.

I sat down next to her; she kissed me, not on the cheek as she used to do, but on the mouth.

'Hello, stranger.' She turned to Ralph on her other side. 'Remember Tom?'

'Of course I remember Tom.' He smiled at me.

'He's a bit of a shit, is Tom.' Her voice was a little slurred. 'One of Nature's fascists, is Tom. Doesn't remember his old friends now. Hasn't bothered to see me for six years . . .'

'You're a bit hard on me,' I said.

'No harder than you deserve, you bugger. You're a cold little sod, Tom, I always said you were. Have a drink now you're here, though. Everyone have a drink . . .'

Ralph whispered in her ear.

'I don't give a toss,' she said. 'Don't be such a bloody

old woman.' She pressed the bell. 'Ralph watches the rounds, Tom. Very bourgeois trick, that. Afraid I'll be exploited.'

There was an awkward silence.

'How's Max?' I asked.

She laughed. 'Got a girl friend. Doesn't know I know. I think it's the last flare-up of his prostate myself.'

'Shush,' Ralph said.

'Don't shush me in front of my friends,' she said sharply. She put a finger under my chin. 'I wonder why I never fancied you? Too bloody cold, that's why . . . You don't want me to shush, do you? Because you're taking notes, aren't you, my little Frankenstein monster?'

I did take notes, but I haven't used them until now. I stayed until closing-time, when I helped Ralph take her to his car. She was staggering a little, which wasn't surprising considering the amount of Scotch she'd consumed.

She stopped at the car – it was an old Ford Popular, I remember, one of the few small cars in which a top hat could be worn.

'I've said some nasty things to you tonight,' she said.

'Don't let that worry you.'

'I want it to worry *you*. You're getting too bloody slick. You're in there making it with the images, cool and above – above – above it all!' She belched. 'But where the bloody hell are *you*? Where's the human being? Who and what do you care for?'

I had had enough. I don't really know how I had stood so much all evening with the new Gang, the new strange Gang, listening fascinated as she'd told them and anyone else in the room who cared to listen, about how much I owed to her, how I'd avoided her all these years, how she'd got me out of the mess with Cora, how false my work had become – there had been all this and much more, and I had sat there and taken it because I felt that in a sense I owed it to her, that I deserved some kind of punishment. But I had reached my limit. If I'd felt any guilt when I entered the Coble, I was certain that now I'd expiated it. If Miranda had apologized, if she'd spoken one friendly word, I should have been disarmed. I should have forgiven her. But this final attack was too much; anger took over and I found myself shouting at her: 'Who the hell are you to talk, you bloody has-been? I earn a living from my writing, don't I? What good are you except to get pissy-eyed with a gang of cadgers and have it off with that double-doored old creep there?'

Miranda stared at me for a minute then slapped my face. Then she was violently sick; Ralph put his arm round her waist to hold her up. Two of the Gang stood nearby, their mouths open. Neither could have been more than nineteen; they were identically dressed in grey flannels and navy blue blazers and white open-neck shirts. I walked straight towards them, my fists clenched, and they made way for me.

It was when I was on the train back to London on the Sunday that the idea for my first novel came to me. It had nothing to do with the scene at the Coble the night before; but without the scene at the Coble the idea wouldn't have come to me. The whole plot didn't present itself to me ready-made; but I could see two main characters, the woman in her forties and the young man in his twenties. Miranda wasn't the woman and I wasn't the man; but the emotion between us that evening at the Coble was of the intensity the novel needed.

By the time I reached King's Cross I had half a dozen pages of notes and a very rough outline of a story: the young man would destroy the older woman and in so doing would destroy himself, the setting would be a small town, but it wouldn't be Engelsea, and somewhere a younger woman would be involved. As I went into the Tube I was already rummaging through my storehouse for the reels marked Cora and Jane. It was as simple and fortuitous, and as contrived and complex, as that, it was based upon my experience and was in no way a direct transcription of my experience.

It was published in 1964, when I'd left *Vanguard* for the *Argus,* and shortly before my marriage to Jean Pitlochry, who wrote for the Woman's Page. Jean was oddly – or not perhaps so oddly, since every man has a preferred sexual type – like Cora, except that she had a slight Scottish accent and was rather fuller in the figure. She was highly articulate, rather Left-Wing, and much in demand on TV and radio; she wasn't a big Name, but she was nevertheless a Name, used to being made a fuss of, to being mildly lionized. Of the two of us, up to the publication of my novel, she was the better known; had it remained like that, we should no doubt have still been married. My novel altered all that. I was now not only a big Name, but an international big Name, and I was honoured a good deal beyond my deserts. (There weren't many other readable novels that year.)

And I continued to be a big Name; the film of the novel continued my success story and my second and third novels were respectable sellers. None of this has any connection with my merits as a writer; the point is that Jean, after a lifetime of being top of the class right from her primary school, found herself almost overnight only occupying that position by the fact of being my wife. Even the birth of Giles made no difference; the Pressmen who flocked to the nursing home were interested in Tom Metfield's wife, not Jean Pitlochry.

Our divorce – five years after our marriage – was inevitable. The co-respondent was Bob Dunsforth, an amiable young director of a family engineering firm. The real co-respondent, as I've already said, was my work. And there was Miranda, however much I may have pushed her into the back of my mind; because of what she had taught me I was a husband and father merely in the physical sense. I was on my tod, on the outside looking in, the day I married, and I didn't change. And throughout our courtship – if it can be called that, since on her insistence we lived together for a year before we married – and throughout our marriage and throughout the whole dreary business of divorce I was aware I was going to use her, that our relationship was going to be filed in my storehouse.

Seventeen

What worries me about Deirdre is that I haven't been able to use her. I don't think that I ever will. I can't think about her coolly and I don't think that I'm ever going to be able to. She makes me feel vulnerable in the same way that Amelia made me feel vulnerable, and that Giles would make me feel vulnerable if I let him enter my mind.

It isn't merely sex which attracts me to her; we didn't go to bed together until we'd known each other for two months, and even then it didn't seem all that important. In any case she isn't really my sexual type: inescapably I prefer dark-haired women and always will. She was wrong when she said that Saturday morning in my bedroom that I only wanted her for one thing; the trouble was that she had so much more to give and that I was frightened of taking it. I wonder now if Alec Wallasley didn't have this in mind when he first introduced us. That was at a party at his flat in Hampstead; the flat, a large untidy one crammed with Victorian furniture and bric-à-brac, was my second home after my divorce, and the HQ of a much more successful and sophisticated metropolitan equivalent of Miranda's Gang. There were always more girls than men at the parties there and Alec, a tall and skinny man with a pointed beard who might have been any age between forty and fifty, had a talent for acquiring those dolly girls who were in the news at the moment. I used him as the basis of my hero in my fourth novel; our friendship was never quite the same after that. It wasn't that anyone recognized him; my hero was younger, handsomer, not a divorcé, not a journalist, and not a serious counter-revolutionary theorist with an international reputation.

Our friendship remained, but I had used him and I had used his home and the circle of friends who were in a sense his family. I had betrayed no secrets, publicized no confidences; the book was a work of fiction. But between friends there's a sort of reticence – I cannot get nearer it than that – which I hadn't preserved. Perhaps he brought Deirdre into my life precisely because he knew that I couldn't use her, so that I should be forced into a genuine human relationship for once.

I remember that he was wearing a purple suit and two buttons on his lapel, one inscribed SAY IT AGAIN, SPYRO and the other KILL A COMMIE FOR CHRIST. He looked round the company with a proprietorial air. 'Hand-picked, lad,' he said. 'A bomb in this room and the counter-revolution's over before it's started.' He looked admiringly at a giggle – or whatever the collective term is – of dolly girls in the far corner. 'To use an expression of yours, the trouble with cunt, lad, is that the women have all of it. A very wise saying. Here we have a commodity which is essential to our well-being if not to our sanity. It should be kept under lock and key and only dispensed in limited quantities, on production of a medical certificate. Yet who has charge of it? Illogical, emotional creatures who either hang on to it or issue it to all and sundry . . .' He caught sight of Deirdre's red head. 'Deirdre, here's someone you were wanting to meet.' He smiled. 'She'll be good for you, Tom. I don't know whether you'll be good for her.'

We didn't have the chance to talk very much that evening; she told me that she liked my second novel best of all because it made her cry and the others didn't; and we arranged to lunch at the studio of her TV company to talk about my writing something for them. 'But it's only an excuse to see you again,' she said, leaving me in what was for me an unusual state of pleased embarrassment. She had the same directness as Maurice's wife Maureen, and the same way of seeming to pour vitality into you instead of taking it out.

I didn't take her home; she went off with the dim young man she came with, and I went to bed finally with a girl from South Vietnam who scratched me all down my back and whom I suppose I shall use if ever any of my characters have occasion to go to bed with a girl from South Vietnam. But I lunched with Deirdre and I wrote the play, more to prove to myself that I could do it than out of any urgent creative need.

On the Saturday morning she left my house in a rage I stayed in bed until ten, thinking about Miranda. Then I had a shower and dressed and went into the nearby supermarket in Kensington High Street, still thinking about Miranda.

For once a colourless series of statements is entirely accurate. I have always enjoyed the minor details of living, have in fact come to value them more and more. I enjoy showering, I enjoy shaving, I enjoy having a huge selection of clothes, I enjoy dressing, I enjoy walking along Kensington High Street, and I enjoy choosing food in a supermarket. Normally I would have wanted to note it all, to put down the sensation of the impact of the shower, the colour of the shower curtains, the texture of the towels, to enumerate each suit, each pair of socks, each shirt, each jacket, each tie, each neckerchief, each sweater, each pair of shoes. (I do remember now that I chose a light blue Crimplene jacket in check, a pair of navy blue slacks, a pair of yellow socks, a yellow nylon polo-neck sweater, and a pair of black Bally wet-look casuals.) Normally also I would have wanted to put down the sting of the after shave, the appearance of each passer-by, the details of each building, to have enumerated every item in the super-market, for I would have enjoyed it all, been grateful for it all, and this would have been the only way for me to have praised it all. But that morning my mind was full of Miranda and I only noticed the world outside me briefly when buying salami, bread, butter, duck pâté, Cheshire cheese, tea and coffee in the supermarket. At home in my study I was grateful from time to time for the comfort of the huge leather-covered sofa, switched the 'phone over to the answering service and didn't touch it again until Monday.

On Monday I 'phoned Miranda. A man's voice, deep and hoarse with a slight Yorkshire accent, answered. 'Engelsea 450, who the bloody hell's that? *Who?* Yes, and this is Herbert Bloody Marcuse – ' There was a gasp as if the owner of the voice had been punched, and Miranda's voice came over, 'Tom? Never mind that clown. Where are you?'

'At my London residence.'

'To which I've never been invited.'

'You don't need an invitation. Anyway, I'm coming to see you.'

'It's been a long time, you bastard.'

'Oh God, Miranda, what the hell does it matter?'

'You knew Max was dead?'

'It's two years ago, love. My father told me.'

'You could have written. Not that he was any great loss, but you could have written.' She sounded tearful.

'I won't come if you don't want me to.'

'Oh Christ, come. People tell me you're a right fascist bastard these days.'

'Which people?' I laughed. 'You know I don't have any politics, honey.'

'That's what I mean. See you at the Grange tonight.' She rang off.

Eight hours later I was in Engelsea driving along Filey Road. It had been warm enough when I started to drive with the hood down; but just inside the Yorkshire border a cold east wind had made me stop to put it up. I'd pushed the Morgan up to 120 on the M1; as I drove along the Filey Road my cheeks were still stinging with the wind and the sun. There was a pleasure to be had from driving with the hood up too, even now that I'd slowed down; canvas and Perspex were somehow more adventurous than steel and glass, seemed to bring one more intimately in contact with the elements. The Morgan had been one of the ways in which I celebrated my freedom from Jean; it was a bachelor's car, exactly the sort of car I'd longed for when I was a bachelor but hadn't been able to afford. In its bright orange with its chromium rollbar and its halogen foglamps and long bonnet with nearly 180 horsepower underneath it, it was a glittering status symbol and trendy envy-inducer; it was no doubt rather puerile of me, but I was very glad to be driving up to the Grange in it and I intended to make sure that Miranda wouldn't miss seeing it.

The Grange seemed a little shabbier than when I'd last seen it. There were cracks in the tarmac of the drive, the paintwork was shabby, the lawn wasn't as yet overgrown, but it hadn't been cut regularly. Though it was daylight, the carriage lamps on either side of the door hadn't been turned off. By the courtyard was a battered Volkswagen minibus covered with slogans and transfers – POWER TO THE PEOPLE, LEGALIZE POT, POWER COMES FROM THE MUZZLE OF THE GUN, VICTORY TO THE N.L.F., CHE LIVES!, heads of Lenin, Ché, Mao, guns, grenades, flowers and, of course, the mushroom cloud. The sky was grey now, not pearly as it could sometimes be in this part of the world, but the grey of dirty shoddy; I began to wonder why I'd come.

Ralph Thoralby answered the door; at first I didn't recognize him. He was wearing long sideboards which further elongated his already elongated face; his black trousers were tucked into black boots, and his red neckerchief, fastened with what looked like a golden chain, added a touch of colour to his black shirt. His skin was sallow no longer but an even brown; I speculated upon whether it was no more genuine than the blackness of his hair, which had been speckled with grey when last I saw him.

'Christ!' I said, 'the fastest gun in the West. What do they think of that outfit at the Grammar School, Ralph?'

'I've retired, my dear.' He helped me off with my anorak and ran his hand lightly over my hair, which as everyone grows theirs longer I keep having cut shorter, so that now it's only just long enough to part. 'As butch as ever, I see. Tweed jacket, the good old grey slacks, the Viyella shirt.'

'Protective colouring,' I said. 'I can go anywhere. You can't.'

'I don't want to go *anywhere*, love.'

Full blast from Miranda's study came suddenly *Johnny Reggae,* there was a smell of dust and incense in the hall.

'It used to be Wagner,' I said.

'A lot of things used to be.'

'Does she still go to the Coble?'

He shook his head. I noticed that he wore a silver identity bracelet. 'Too bourgeois. And there was trouble with the management. They don't like students. Not the new kind.'

'New kind?'

'Had you forgotten about our new university?'

'Students,' I said. 'Oh Christ!'

'They're very sweet friendly young people.' He giggled. 'Enlarge your experience, ducky.'

The study was full of people and smoke and the sound of *Johnny Reggae* and voices; it hadn't changed since I last saw it except that there were piles of newspapers and magazines on top of the bookcases, a Sony hi-fi, and a litter of galley proofs, typescripts, and Press photos on the desk. Miranda was wearing a pink linen trouser suit and gold slippers; her face was an even brown like Ralph's but obviously her tan hadn't come out of a bottle. She had worn well, though the flesh at the opening of her jacket was beginning to take on the texture of crepe. Beside her on the sofa a big bearded man of about my age with hair half-down his shoulders leaned back, his eyes closed, his hand resting on her crotch. I bent down and kissed her on the cheek but she put her arms round my neck and kissed me on the lips.

'Tom, it's been so long . . . Sit down, honey. Did you have a good journey?'

She put her hand on my knee; the big bearded man beside her didn't open his eyes or move his hand.

'He has a Morgan Plus Eight now,' Ralph said, fiddling

with the hi-fi control deck, which was black and chrome, with what appeared to be some thirty switches and buttons. 'Bright orange, a real bird-catcher.'

'Conspicuous expenditure,' said the bearded man, his eyes still closed. I recognized the voice which I'd heard on the 'phone that morning. 'Waste of man-hours, waste of irreplaceable fossil fuel, waste of power.'

'You're absolutely right,' I said stifling a genuine yawn.

'You don't want to argue?'

'No.'

'Then fuck you.' His hand had all this time been stroking Miranda's crotch; she seemed not to feel it. 'This is Jim Camarthen,' she said. 'Jim, Tom Metfield. Don't say you haven't heard of him.'

The bearded man opened his eyes and nodded at me. 'I've heard of him. Put a bun in my cousin Cora's oven. Writes decadent bourgeois crap – like you used to write, Miranda.'

'It's a living,' I said. 'I don't really care very much what people think about it.'

'No, you don't.'

Johnny Reggae was displaced by a rhythmic yelling backed by a piano then by drums. The noise mounted; it didn't seem to affect anyone else in the room. 'Switch it off, Ralph,' Jim Camarthen bellowed. 'I hate that bloody wet dream music. The kids like it though.'

Looking around, I saw the others were indeed kids; the oldest there, a tall thin boy in blue jeans and tie-dyed T-shirt and Afro hair-do, wouldn't have been any more than twenty-one. There were six boys and three girls; they were all in drab browns and blacks, the girls in flimsy floor-length dresses. They didn't seem to be aware that I was looking at them.

'The kids are welcome to it,' I said. 'How is Cora?'

'She married a bookie. Wears bloody mink and rides about in a Mercedes now. Always was an aspiring bourgeois. Now she's made it.'

'I'm glad.'

'She's no different from you, except that she's peddled her cunt and you've peddled your talent.'

This annoyed me, I don't know why. 'How's *your* talent?' I asked. 'Any buyers? Or is it buried too deep?'

The boy with the Afro hair-do, another boy with a straggly fair beard, and two of the girls drifted over to the sofa and stood looking at us in silence. Ralph left the now silent hi-fi and stood beside the boy in the Afro hair-do, his hand on his shoulder.

'You mustn't be like that with Jim,' Miranda said sharply. 'He hasn't published in the sort of magazine you read, that's all.' She squeezed Jim's hand. 'He stopped me drinking and started me thinking.' She giggled. 'Rather trite, but good. You knew I was writing another novel? But this will be *committed*. Committed totally to the changing of our rotten society.'

'I'd like to read it.'

'You won't really like it. I've left the world of private sensation . . .'

Suddenly my mind seemed to cut out. Ralph put a glass of whisky in my hand; I sipped it mechanically, aware of Miranda's voice droning relentlessly on about the workers, capitalism, alienation, revolution and, I think, Vietnam. What was literature about, what was art about, if it wasn't about private sensation? If the world was going to change in the way she said it was going to change, what would be the point in my living?

The rest of the students had drifted over to the sofa. They were listening to Miranda – as I suppose I once had listened to her at the Coble. What was important to them was not what she said or that a member of her generation should say it. And she was, in the Methodist phrase, bearing witness against the world, the flesh and the bourgeois devil in the shape of Tom Metfield, though I wasn't as it were manifesting my devilishness but sitting quietly whilst the hoarse voice, still with something compulsively attractive about it, went relentlessly on. She stopped and lit a cigarette and I said mildly: 'The rotten bourgeois society hasn't done badly by you, darling.'

'Because it's so clumsy and capricious and stupid. And I shall use what it's given me to destroy it.'

'We'll establish a commune,' the young man with the Afro hair-do said. 'We'll issue pamphlets, a real Socialist newspaper, we'll publish books, we'll stage plays, we'll have happenings . . .'

'Good luck to you,' I said. 'Miranda, I'm rather tired. Couldn't we get together some other time?'

A girl in a brown dress with a rather pretty face looked at me as if she wanted to hit me. 'Christ, you are a decadent shit, aren't you? Don't you care? Don't you care one way or the other? Don't you have any bloody reactions at all?'

'I'm neutral. I'm just a writer, just a worn-out old hack.'

'Worn-out old hack be buggered. I've read your books. Miranda taught you how to write, she wouldn't have wasted her time on a hack.'

'I'm neutral, dear. And bloody tired, and I've heard it all before.'

'You're bloody soft, you're bloody dead!' She was shouting now. 'Don't you have any answers?'

I thought of Alec Wallasley; he would have said *I hope I live to see you hanged,* and have meant it. But he was a soldier and I was a war correspondent, an accredited non-combatant.

'There is an answer,' I said. 'You'll find out one day.

But it won't be in words.' I don't know why I said it, and am still asking myself why. But when I'd said it there was silence. 'Miranda, I really am shagged-out. I'll 'phone you.' I stood up.

She pulled me down beside her and gestured to the students; suddenly they weren't there and Jim had closed his eyes again. 'You're out of touch, aren't you, Tom?' she asked gently.

'I expect so.'

'Tom, you just want an easy life and no-one's going to have an easy life any more. You want to celebrate the bourgeois world – '

'Celebrate, yes. It's odd you should choose that word – '

'Oh God, that's the point. It's there in all your stuff, it always was. You don't celebrate at a deathbed. It's dying, your lovely bourgeois world, it started to die in 1917. Something big's happening, Tom. *That*'s what you should celebrate. Oh yes, these kids here are ignorant little twots, but they know the score and you don't. You should care about what's happening, Tom, you should be writing about it. I'm writing about it. I've come to life again, do you understand?'

She took a handful of Jim's long hair – it was nearly down to the middle of his back – and pulled his head round to face her. He opened his eyes; they were grey-blue and bloodshot. 'He's only intermittently good as a poet and he stinks like a whore's armpits, but he started me writing again.'

He struck her hand away and leaned back, closing his eyes again. 'Leave me alone, fuck you. I'm thinking.' His hand returned to Miranda's crotch.

'Will it be a novel?' I asked.

'Oh Jesus, you don't speak in those terms. The form doesn't matter, you cram everything in. You're taking action, you're joining the war. I thought the Communists had the answer once – that was when Harvey was a member. Used to subscribe to Party funds on the quiet . . .'

'Do you still?'

'Tom, don't you know anything? We go on from Marx, they go on from Stalin. They think they're using us, but we use them. They'll have to go in the end, but first of all, your bourgeois world has to go. Before you build the new city, you pull the old one down. It's all in my book, it'll be the best thing I've ever done . . .'

I was trying to keep the tears back. They were tears for the world of my youth that had seemed so secure, they were tears for the Miranda's Gang I'd known – Miranda's Gang, Mark 1. I saw now that on my last visit it had been replaced by Mark 2. I hadn't liked that, but it had still been recognizably the derivation of Mark 1. But Mark 3 was different again. Its function was to destroy my bourgeois world, past and present, my kind, gentle, beautiful bourgeois world that had every virtue but the will to live. 'Yes, it'll be a good book, Miranda,' I said. 'You're a good writer.'

'I've worked it all out,' she said, stroking Jim's hair absently. 'Society silenced me. I lost my integrity. I was thinking as an individual, I wasn't thinking historically. I lost my talent because I didn't realize what it was *for*. And now I've got it back.'

'I'm sure you've never lost it.' I still wanted to weep, but another part of me was watching and listening, cold and dry-eyed.

'Yes, I've got it back,' she said. 'But what did I do to you? I turned you into a successful bourgeois. Damn you, you're not even a reactionary bourgeois. You haven't even the guts to be a fascist bastard. You don't give a damn, do you?'

That was a good question, I thought. Was I so much part of that world that I'd lost my will to live too?

'No, Miranda, I don't give a damn. Politics bores me stiff. I'm just a writer.'

Something about her seemed to slacken. 'You shouldn't – ' she whispered. For a second she seemed all of her sixty years, her face a chaos of deep lines.

I looked at her with a helpless love. 'Shouldn't what, Miranda?'

Her face was taut again. 'Nothing, darling. Have another drink.'

I shook my head and got up. My desire to weep had left me. I kissed her forehead; it was very dry and hot.

'I'll see you.'

She didn't answer; as I went out of the room Ralph left the young man with the Afro hair-do and put his hand on my arm.

'I'm sorry you had a rough passage.'

'It might be rougher for you than for me in the end.'

He smiled. 'My dear, they're surprisingly tolerant. They really are all for doing your own thing, as they put it. Don't be sorry for me.'

'I'm just a little puzzled. This isn't really your scene, is it?'

His hand still on my arm, he led me into the hall and picked up my anorak.

'It's better than being lonely,' he said, helping me into the anorak. He opened the door; it was still light, but there was a faint red glow in the west. The wind was very cold. I was aware that I was being shown out, that he'd been given his orders without a word being spoken, but he was a link with the past I didn't want to break, he spoke a language which I might not hear again.

'What about her sons?' I asked.

'They're in London. Young Max is a barrister. Donald's an accountant. They were never very – *close*.' He frowned, holding the door open. 'It really is cold, darling.'

I went through the door, then turned as he was about to shut it.

'Ralph, will you give Miranda a message for me?'

'Make it short, pet, my balls are frozen off me.'

'She has the book . . . Power, to his companion Force and to their prisoner Prometheus – wait, Ralph – Power says: We have come to the last path of the world, in the Scythian country, in the untrodden solitude . . .'

'Very pretty.' He giggled. 'You're a fool, Tom. I never liked you.' He slammed the door shut.

Eighteen

When I returned to Kensington I was seized with apathy.
I opened no letters, kept the 'phone switched on to the
answering service, and did no work, lying in bed all
morning, wandering about Kensington all afternoon, and
lying on the sofa in the study all evening; I drank no
alcohol because for some reason it seemed necessary to
keep my mind clear. I suppose that what I really did was
to hole up, to go to earth, to lick my wounds in my cosy
little burrow.

It was unseasonably cold that May, with summer clothes
piling up unwanted in the shops and pictures of deserted
beaches in the papers, which helped to add to a pervading
sense of unreality which I couldn't shake off and didn't
want to try. My house was in what estate agents describe
as a favoured area of Kensington near St Mary Abbott's
in a terrace built in the 1880s. It was in stone with a
narrow front, unusually plain for the period, its only
ornament a ridiculous little balcony on the first floor;
I was very fond of it but began to have the feeling that
when I opened the front door there would be a black
void behind it: this only lasted a split second but left me
a little shaken after it had gone. And sometimes I would
anticipate before going into my study that it would have
someone in it whom I would not wish to see. Lying on the

sofa I would see it as a facsimile of Miranda's study at the Grange; it would again be a split second before I came back to normal, realized that it was half the size, that the wallpaper and carpet were orange and yellow, that there were yellow Venetian blinds and not curtains, that there was a Victorian davenport instead of a massive mahogany desk and photos of my father and mother and Amelia instead of the portrait of Miranda. I wasn't, as they say, losing my marbles; it was simply that at the hands of Miranda and her new Gang I'd had the same beating-up psychologically as I'd once had physically from Cora's father. And just as I'd recovered from that beating-up so I recovered from this.

It was on the fourth evening after my return from Engelsea; I was lying half asleep on the study sofa when suddenly I was awake and on my feet, walking over to the 'phone in almost the same movement, and calling Deirdre. I had let go, I had relaxed, I had rested; I was going forward now, certainly not in the assurance of victory, but forward and not alone. There was no answer; I stood staring at Amelia's photo for a few moments, then went back to the 'phone and asked for International Service.

Amelia had become a nurse after leaving school, married a young doctor in Scarborough, and they'd emigrated to Canada a year after they married. She'd grown up tall and leggy, with a thin, lively face and tranquil eyes; I hadn't seen her since she'd emigrated and that, I realized with a shock, was four years ago.

Her voice was high, eager, slightly breathless, with a slight Yorkshire accent; it hadn't changed, and what I felt for her hadn't changed.

'I'm coming to see you,' I said.

'Lovely! When?'

'Next week.'

'Are you on a lecture tour?'

'I'm just coming to see you. And Simon. And the twins.'

'I tell them about you. How clever you are. And how you used to tell stories to me when I was a little girl . . . Oh, Tom, I'm so happy you're coming, I could cry – '

'Don't do that, doy,' I said, feeling close to tears myself. 'I'll 'phone you again tomorrow, and we'll arrange the details.'

'Oh, Tom, it's so lovely. I can't believe it.'

'I should have come before,' I said.

'It doesn't matter, Tom, I know you're so busy. Tom, has anything happened?'

'In a way. Nothing unpleasant, love, just a change. I'll tell you tomorrow.'

I heard footsteps outside, then the creak of the letter-box opening: I said goodbye to Amelia and ran to the front door to see Deirdre walking quickly down the street. I ran after her, still in my slippers, and grabbed her arm.

'Get off me,' she said. 'I've finished with you.'

'But *I* haven't finished with you.'

'If you don't let go my arm I'll scream.'

'I've been trying to get you on the 'phone.'

'Only now, is it? I know how long you've been back. I saw your car four days ago.'

I released her arm. 'Come on. I can't talk to you out here.'

She rubbed her arm. 'I'll do the talking. You're the most selfish, self-centred, conceited, cold-hearted bastard I've ever met in all my born days, and that's just a start . . .'

A very old woman – Kensington is full of very old women – had stopped muttering to herself and was listening intently.

'Do come on,' I said. 'That old girl's turning up her deaf aid.'

'I don't care,' Deirdre said. 'I'd just like you to be shown up . . . What the hell are you smiling about?'

'I'm happy.'

She looked at me intently for a minute, then smiled, and we both went into the house. The old woman pulled a face and walked off in the opposite direction, muttering to herself again.

She didn't speak again until we were in the study:

'Why are you happy?' she asked.

I put my hands gently to her cheeks. They were cold, but also, in a way I can't explain, radiated warmth.

'I think I feel better with you here than not here. I might even love you.'

'Thank you. You have a damned queer way of showing it.'

'I'm too old to change.' I took her coat off: she was wearing a green jersey wool mini-dress. 'Come to bed.'

She moved away from me. 'You with all your money – and you can't afford a calendar.'

'It doesn't matter. Just sit beside me a minute.'

'You've been to see Miranda, haven't you?'

I nodded.

'What happened?'

'I'll tell you about it later. Make some tea, I'm fed up with making my own.'

'Did you enjoy seeing her?'

'No.'

'You put it off too long. There's someone else whom you should see, isn't there? Are you going to put that off?'

'I've just 'phoned her.'

'When are you going to see her?'

'Soon.'

'When's soon?'

'I'll arrange it with her tomorrow.'

'You won't, you know. You'll put it off.'

'Make me some tea and stop nagging.'

'Promise me to arrange it tomorrow then.'

'I've told you. I'll do it tomorrow.'

'I don't trust you. God, you're an awful man. You talk about loving people – how the hell can you love them if you don't see them? Why didn't you arrange it when you 'phoned her?'

'Oh, stop nagging. You haven't been here five minutes and you're bloody nagging. I hate nagging women.'

She stood up. 'I'll go then.'

'No,' I said. 'You may as well stay.'

'I'm going to make the tea,' she said.

I thought I heard her crying in the kitchen but when she returned I could see no traces of it on her face.

'I want us to move from here,' she said.

I stroked her hand. 'If that's what you want, I suppose that's settled it.'

'It's too much the bachelor's den. Not the place for children. And I've been thinking about Giles. It's not right for you not to see him.'

'Oh God,' I said, 'where will you stop?'

'If you don't see him regularly then one day you'll just *have* to see him. And then you'll be hurt. Like you were when you saw Miranda. You just pick people up, Tom, and then put them down. You don't see them for years and you expect them not to change. You'll have to see Miranda again, Tom. Else you won't remember her. Not properly remember her, not remember her as she really is.'

Deirdre was right and Deirdre was wrong. I shall

see her again but even if I don't see her again I shall remember her. If I don't remember her, I shall remember nothing else, I shall cease to be a writer – for what else is writing but remembering, waking from the dream to seize the pen from the bedside? I don't want to end the story at this point, I want to go back into the dream. But I know that I won't go back into the same dream. And perhaps it's best that it should be so, because this dream is full of danger. The truth takes me too deep. Another dive and my lungs would burst. All right for some; it wouldn't be *your* lungs, would it? And so I end the story.

But after I've ended it, there that town by the sea still is, there Miranda still is, an old woman now, still queen of a country which seems to me increasingly distant with the passing of time and the change of our philosophies, but still with the same authority, still with – there's no other word for it – the same magic. I find her new court less than dazzling and her new creed harsh and deadly, but that's of no account. She won't finish her book, but that's of no account either. I believe that I've progressed further than she, that my kingdom is larger, because I have given up more, am even now prepared to give up as much again. And I say that having more, having more when I least expected it, surprised by love when I had almost expected to live without it.

That's a separate consideration. It isn't a judgement upon her. Nor has it anything to do with pity. For I love Miranda and I always will. She and I share the same secret, even if we haven't fully comprehended it, even if – because of the limitations of our species rather than of our aspirations – we never will.